Edward Augustus Rand

A Knight that Smote the Dragon

Or the Young People's Gough

Edward Augustus Rand

A Knight that Smote the Dragon
Or the Young People's Gough

ISBN/EAN: 9783337269982

Printed in Europe, USA, Canada, Australia, Japan

Cover: Foto ©Andreas Hilbeck / pixelio.de

More available books at **www.hansebooks.com**

JOHN B. GOUGH.

A KNIGHT

THAT

SMOTE THE DRAGON

OR

THE YOUNG PEOPLE'S GOUGH

BY

EDWARD A. RAND

AUTHOR OF

Deeds Worth Telling, Art Series, Under the Lantern at Black Rocks,
The Drummer-Boy of the Rappahannock, Sailor-Boy Bob,
When the War Broke Out, Look Ahead Series,
School and Camp Series, Margie
at the Harbor Light, etc.

NEW YORK: HUNT & EATON
CINCINNATI: CRANSTON & STOWE

PREFACE.

THE late John B. Gough, the great temperance orator of his day, told in a little volume (1845) the story of his youth, his descent into the midnight depths of intemperance, and his painful ascent into liberty and the light again. The details of his subsequent life have been given in other volumes, but that first little book of 1845 holds for the most part the facts that I specially wish to emphasize for the sake of our young people. These facts make a glass through which we can look back and see what unmade Gough and then made him. Here we find the warning against wrong and the spur to reformation. I would add that in a fitting memorial issued by the National Temperance Society, that noble organization, I found a helpful summary of facts and addresses from which I have been kindly allowed to quote. The life of Gough gives a summons to all to move upon that beastly, cruel enemy, Drink. If under the Dragon's foot to-day, let not any despair. In the strength of God, may they rise like Gough and deal that wound of death which will be the healing of their own hurt!

CONTENTS.

A KNIGHT THAT SMOTE THE DRAGON;

OR,

THE YOUNG PEOPLE'S GOUGH.

CHAPTER I.

WHERE WAS HE BORN?

DO you use an atlas much? One advantage is this—it makes traveling very cheap. If you keep your atlas within reaching-distance, it is like a locomotive and cars ever waiting at your door, the steam up and fizzing, the train ready at your bidding to take you wherever you say. In the present case, as we wish to go across the water, a train of cars will not serve us. We must therefore use wings. Our atlas resting on the shelf shall become a pair of wings. This very moment they shall be attached to our shoulders and we will fly away—to Europe. Here we are, without any fuss, without any expense, off Land's End, England, and flying up the English Channel. One second more and we are in the Strait of Dover. Now look off upon the coast of Kent, where the big bulging cliffs seem very much like huge fists doubled up and defiantly held out toward all the continent and France in particular. We look along the white, foam-fringed coast. Deal? That is not the place we want. Dover? Folkstone? No. Sandgate? Yes. It is an attractive watering-place for puffing, panting Englishmen who hurry out of the cities in the warm summer-time; and some of them doubtless make a great stir when they arrive. One August day, the 22d, far back in the year 1817, there came to Sandgate a very important personage, judging by the amount of bustle and stir in one house. This individual was a baby. It was a brave soldier's baby. The name given to him was that of John Bartholomew Gough. The cradle rocked a soul whose baby-cry was one day destined to develop into the eloquent voice that would echo up and down the land, warning men against intemperance and winning them to a life of abstinence, joy, and thrift.

It is always of interest in the early life of men and women to ascertain what circumstances helped make them. Here at Sandgate was a

child destined to move big England and still
bigger America. What helped make the soldier's boy running about Sandgate's old-fashioned
streets a child among the children trooping
every-where? Was there any thing of remark-
able interest in his character and life? Lively,
enthusiastic, fond of fun, what was there of particular note in the boy himself or his surroundings? I emphasize this point because our early
life points forward to our manhood or woman-
hood. There was something in John Gough's
home and surroundings looking toward the future and uttering its prophecy.

There are peculiarities of your present life that
will make useful material to be worked up into
an honorable and effective future. What about
the Sandgate boy down by the sea? He had a
very sensitive temperament and a keen imagination, and I can see how powerful in their influence must have been certain conditions of his
childhood. There was the sea, vast, mysterious,
ever shouting on the beach its great chorus of
unrest. John Gough would go to the beach and
there watch this vast, fascinating, restless sea.
When he was a man speaking to and swaying
great audiences he could go in thought to the

sea-shore and find in those great, stretching waters the material for a vivid illustration, or recall a story told by some bronzed old seaman.

The shores of the English Channel have seen many wrecks. A famous one was that of the *Royal George*, a British man-of-war, that suddenly sank in Portsmouth harbor in the year 1782. In those days when they wished to make repairs on the lower part of a vessel's hull the custom was to "heel her over." This meant to throw her over on one side, and it was a delicate operation. Alas! the *Royal George* received too much of a tip. The water flowed into the port-holes of the side thus borne down, and she quickly sank. At the time she had on board eleven hundred people, and of these three hundred were women and children. The greater number of this living cargo of the *Royal George* found a silent, shadowy grave in Portsmouth harbor. This accident sent a shiver of horror all through England, and the poet Cowper, when he heard the news, wrote lines that you must have already read:

> "Toll for the brave!
>   The brave that are no more!
> All sunk beneath the wave,
>   Fast by their native shore!

"Eight hundred of the brave,
    Whose courage well was tried,
Had made the vessel heel,
    And laid her on her side.

"A land breeze shook the shrouds,
    And she was overset;
Down went the *Royal George*,
    With all her crew complete.

"Toll for the brave!
    Brave Kempenfelt is gone;
His last sea-fight is fought,
    His work of glory done."

These and the remaining lines I fancy that I can hear John Gough reading in the school of his boyhood, not far from those waters of the Channel covering so many hopes that would never live and bloom again. The sea fringed the boy's life with an element of the tragic and awful. It kept alive and developed within him the sense of the abrupt and venturous. It aroused the quality of the heroic when the saving of life at sea was the supreme question of the hour. Any time, by day or night, the great ocean might have a caprice of wrath, and a wreck might turn half a dozen prosy Sandgaters into half a dozen magnificent heroes.

Then there was an old castle in Sandgate. It was built by King Henry the Eighth. Among

those who had visited it were foremost people
of England.   John knew the keeper of the old
castle, and was allowed to ramble about it whenever he pleased.   There he goes, stealing through
a rough gate-way, slipping down a shadowy
court-yard, or ascending the castle wall and
peering out among the openings in some battle-
ment.   As he went through the stern old gate-
way he may have thought what gay cavaliers
once rode where he walked.   Up on the castle
wall, he may have wondered if Queen Bess stood
there and looked off across the sea to catch a
glimpse of any hostile vessel from Spain.   In
some chamber or hall he may have fancied
Henry the Eighth laughing and jesting with a
knot of courtiers, or he saw the king riding out
over the drawbridge and heard the hoofs of the
horses of his body-guard pounding out a rough,
energetic tune of war.   Would the boy, filling
up the empty air with pictures of brave knights,
ever be himself God's knight in a holy cause?
We shall see.   The old castle had its influence.

A person who fostered, perhaps unconsciously,
the soldierly, combative element in the boy was
his father, that old soldier who had heard the
loud, echoing guns of Corunna and Talavera,

Salamanca and Badajos, Pombal and Busaco. John would deck himself with pieces of the old soldier's equipments, seize and shoulder a broomstick, and then his father would drill him. What boy or girl has not read Charles Wolfe's spirited lines describing the Burial of Sir John Moore?

> "Not a drum was heard, nor a funeral note,
> As his corse to the rampart we hurried;
> Not a soldier discharged his farewell shot
> O'er the grave where our hero we buried."

Moore commanded at the ever-famous engagement of Corunna, a sea-port in Spain, where, with about fourteen thousand men, he beat back twenty thousand French under Soult, who tried to stop the embarkation of the English. Moore won victory and—death. Hurriedly he was buried on a bastion by the shore. The poet says:

> "We buried him darkly at dead of night,
> The sods with our bayonets turning;
> By the struggling moonbeam's misty light,
> And the lantern dimly burning."

The poetry has become celebrated. Its very movement suggests the tramp, tramp of marching men, going out in the night to do some sad work of war. Gough's father was under Moore,

and saw his brave but helpless commander borne
away from the fight. He told his boy about
that death and the dark, lonely burial of the sol-
dier-hero, and the boy's flashing eyes proved how
interested and excited a listener the veteran had.
The latter did not know in what holy battle that
boy would one day engage.

CHAPTER II.

STILL A BOY.

IN finding out the influences that in early life tend to shape character we must not fail to count in "father" and "mother." John Gough's father, the grave veteran, was arousing within the boy a daring, combative element. John Gough's mother was just a warm-hearted, loving woman. Intellectually she must have gone ahead of many in her walk in life. For twenty years she was the village "school-marm." She was a stimulating force in the boy's mental culture. John was not to be limited to the opportunities that Sandgate could afford. He was sent to a "seminary" at Folkstone. He went forward so rapidly in his studies that he was admitted to the rank of instructor! This venerable pedagogue was asked to instruct two classes. One he guided beyond that difficult place in the rugged way of learning, a knowledge of the science of spelling words of two syllables! To another and more experienced set of travelers

he taught the "Rule of Three!" He did not
himself advance very far in his studies, for at
the age of ten he quit school, and forever. That
was a small pack of knowledge which he took
away for life's travels, the scanty accumulations
up to the age of ten! We can make no more
serious mistake than to go out into life with a
slender pack of knowledge. Yes, worse still is
the disposition to be content with our small
stores and never to add to them. John Gough
saw his need, painfully felt it, in after years.
Doubtless if he had been other than a poor
boy he would have been kept at school. The
"seminary" at Folkstone burdened John
Gough's father with an expense his weak pocket-
book could not easily carry. Poor? Yes, the
Goughs were poor. That wolf, poverty, left
some deep scars on the little family circle. Once
their need was very great. The wolf I have
mentioned was snarling more threateningly than
ever. John's mother was not only "school-
ma'am," but lace-maker also. Once when the
wolf was scratching at the door, and money must
be had somehow, the mother walked over eight
miles to Dover, taking her lace with her. She
patiently, wearily tried to find a customer, but

sad, hungry, tired, she was compelled after an unsuccessful day to return home. Seventeen miles for nothing! Seventeen miles for worse than nothing, bringing back a sharp hunger, weary feet, and an aching heart. That was the very day that John happened to come home rich and happy as five shillings and sixpence can make a poor boy. It was money that had been presented to him after an exhibition of his skill in reading. He found his mother crying sadly. She told him how unsuccessful she had been, when to her astonishment he pulled out his treasures and gave them to her. The now happy mother fell upon her knees, John falling with her, and her soul was like a fountain running over with thankfulness to God.

I have been looking at the surroundings of the boy-life in Sandgate to see if any of them could have been sources of power, and so have given strength to coming years. I have spoken of the poverty of the Goughs. It may sound like a contradiction to say that want can be the source of affluence, and yet because John Bartholomew Gough was once a poor boy it gave him in after years the ability to reach down to the poor, to feel for them, to understand them and be a blessing to

2

them. Charles Dickens, the famous author, was
once a poor boy. He is described, at one point
of his life in London, as "carrying things to the
pawn-brokers, visiting his father in the Marshal-
sea" (a kind of prison), "into which the poor
man and his family soon drifted, tying up pots
of blacking at the warehouse, prowling about
cook-shops, alamode beef-shops, and coffee-
shops, a shabbily clad and insufficiently fed little
boy." It has been shown how this experience
was fitting Dickens for his work. Poverty,
then, may be riches. If you are poor, don't say
it is a valueless experience. Don't throw it away
as the part of your life which is an empty vessel. It may hold rich treasure. I have called
poverty a wolf that scarred. Behind the scars,
though, may be any thing but a wolf's teeth. I
only label it "wolf" because poverty may seem
so at the time. It hurts just then, and yet in
later years, looking back upon the hurt, we may
interpret it differently. It may be the spur to
a noble effort. Marryatt says, "A smooth sea
never made a skilled mariner, neither do uninterrupted prosperity and success qualify for usefulness and happiness. The storms of adversity,
like those of the ocean, rouse the faculties and

excite the invention, prudence, skill, and forti-
tude of the voyager." You may look back upon
want and see in it a motive-power urging you
on to success, and thank God for it.

When we look back at the boy-life of Gough,
as he stands there on Sandgate beach, soon to em-
bark on life's perilous voyage, you will not find
his chest rich in its outfit of worldly goods.
Poor boys' chests, though, may become rich
men's coffers. But, in examining the peculiar
conditions of young Gough's life, in turning up
the soil into which it thrust its roots, let us not
overlook that element of prayer contributed to
it by John Gough's parents. In his younger
days he could not appreciate the value of that
prayerful example, but it had its worth. It entered as an unconscious influence into his character. Especially did his mother, a woman of
warm, sincere trust in God, stamp deep upon her
boy's mind the lesson of our spiritual need and
prayer's power. From such a fountain-head of
influence as I have mentioned, that venturous-
ness and daring which a life by the sea and
amid the old historic traditions of Sandgate
Castle would naturally provoke, that aggressive-
ness and courage aroused by his father's career

as a soldier, that sympathy for the hungry and
needy that our hunger and need are sure to
quicken—what kind of a character would be
likely to issue? Would it not be a life feeling
for those oppressed by any evil, and likely to
ride upon and fight the evil out of the way?
In such a fight would not the child of praying
parents be likely to reach up and take hold of
God's hand? We shall see.

But, while it is interesting to trace a life to
its start and notice what helped give it a set
and flow, it is interesting to hunt for any youth-
ful sign of that future greatness. Young people do not understand that their early days carry
the bud of the flower they may give to the world
in the future. Some one remarked of an acquaintance that in his college-life there were the
potency and promise of the man that he would
make in after days. It was a distinguished manhood thus developed. You know it not to-day,
if still young, but there is something about you
inevitably indicating what you will be by and
by. There is some good bud on your branch,
some fair promise in your life. It will be lam-
entable if you make a mistake—if, by the frost
of any careless living to-day you blight to-mor-

row's flower. What about that wide-awake, impulsive, excitable boy, John Gough, running about the streets of Sandgate? Did he have any mental gift that gave promise of power in after life? Any one that ever heard Mr. Gough knows that he had unusual powers in the delineation of character. He showed this talent when a boy. We have seen or must have heard of that popular street-exhibition of Punch and Judy. It had its origin in Italy about the year 1600. It traveled to England, and was specially popular in Queen Anne's reign. If we ever saw Punch's long nose protruding from his show-box on any of our streets we can never forget the sight. John Gough was fascinated by the comical Punch. Out of a chair that was minus its bottom he made a Punch-and-Judy box. The same hands that contrived the box made a Punch and Judy for it. Then he would exhibit these wonders to the boys and girls, and with his power to mimic character he furnished an entertaining exhibition for his grinning, eager-eyed auditors. John had a sister, Mary. She would help him in other efforts of his impersonating genius. He turned a chair into a pulpit. His sister manufactured an audience out

of rag-dolls. Then, personating a clergyman,
John would address his ragged congregation.
In the possession of a power to express character,
to forget that he was John Gough, and, entering into another's feelings, become for a while
that person, he was shadowing forth his far-away
future life as a king of the platform.

Not only in the above, but in reading also, he
showed that he had a gift above the average.
Go over to the wonderful seminary at Folkstone,
where the boy-teacher has instructed his pupils
and now takes his turn as scholar. He stands
up in the reading-class. You hear his liquid,
musical, sympathetic voice giving so easily the
passing thought in the mind of the writer. In
all this was readily suggested what he might ac-
complish through his voice if cultivated.

When very young he gained a reputation as
a reader. Of those early days one pleasant
memento was connected with the distinguished
William Wilberforce. This foremost man is
remembered in English history in connection
with the abolition of the accursed slave-trade.
Wilberforce was born in 1759. When a youth-
ful student he sent a communication to a York
paper in which he denounced the " odious traffic

in human flesh." At that early day he was proph-
esying what he might attempt in adult years.
In 1788, though his health was poor, he conse-
crated himself to an arduous work, and began a
famous crusade against the slave-trade. Year
after year this champion in Parliament fought in
behalf of the slave. Finally, one day, Parliament came round to his side and voted against
the slave-trade. Sir Samuel Romilly, an ally of
Wilberforce, in a speech before Parliament, con-
trasted Napoleon, then in the full tide of success,
and Wilberforce, who would "that day lay his
head upon his pillow and remember that the slave-
trade was no more." There was a breaking out
into applause all over the house, and hearty cheers
went up for the courageous Wilberforce. For
weary years he had laid his head upon his pillow,
as an unsuccessful crusader, nights enough to
merit this sweet repose of victory. Wilberforce
was not satisfied. He still leveled his lance at any
outbreak of the slave-traffic, and he also aimed
to rout slavery itself every-where under the
British flag. No short fight, so much money was
invested in slavery, and behind the money-bags
was the greed of the human heart. He could not
stay in Parliament to wage this fight, so broken was

his health. He retired in 1825. Buxton, a good crusader, took up the fight, and he was permitted to see the flag of this righteous cause triumphant. That was in July, 1833. What a protracted, persistent fight! Wilberforce died the 29th day of that month. Three days before he went home to his reward they brought him the good tidings that the Abolition Bill had passed a second reading. Grateful was Wilberforce. He lifted his soul in thanksgiving to God for the sacrifices that Englishmen had offered in behalf of this cause, twenty millions sterling having been spent. Let us now go back of this period. It was to Sandgate down by the cool sea that the aged Wilberforce was accustomed to come in summer, and John Gough went with his father to the house where Wilberforce was stopping and where a circle had gathered for prayer. Wilberforce noticed John. He gave the boy a book, and in it he wrote John's name. He asked John to read, which he did, and Wilberforce spoke very kindly of the performance. When Wilberforce laid his hand on that boy's head he did not know he was touching in silent bless-ing one who would conduct a glorious crusade against Drink's hard, cruel slavery. As the months went on, John's reputation as a reader did not lessen. People in the street would stop to listen to him as he read to his mother sitting near the cottage door. Sometimes he would be sent for and requested to read. Once a gentleman gave him five shillings for his acceptable reading. Another person laid a sixpence on top of that. It was this money that relieved the want of John's mother after her long, hard walk to Dover and back, in vain trying to sell her lace.

But John Gough's boy-life was rapidly hurrying away. He loved fun, and it sometimes made him trouble. He was very quick to see the humorous side of any event. I can hear his voice ringing out in happy laughter, while his ready mimicry provokes others to a laughter as eager and careless. From May-day in the spring to Guy Fawkes' day in the autumn and then past the bright Christmas and Easter festivals to May-day again, he is just a fun-loving English boy. I catch the echoes of his Punch and Judy exhibitions, or he gives a very solemn address to Mary Gough's rag-dolls. As I listen, though, the liquid, musical notes are dying away, and soon will cease to sound in Sandgate by the sea.

CHAPTER III.

THE WORLD BEFORE HIM.

THE ship *Helen* is drifting out of the Thames, bound for America. The wind swells her snowy sails. As they pull on the ropes the sailors' song echoes over the water. The captain energetically strides the deck and shouts his orders. There are passengers aboard, and they have crept out of the cabin and lean over the rails. But whose is that boy-face turned eagerly toward the sea? That is John Gough, bound for another continent. He is only twelve. That is an early age at which to gather up one's possessions, leave home, cross the sea, find a new world, and there begin life in earnest. It seems altogether too soon for the shutting down of the misty horizon-line upon the boy-life at Sandgate, on father, mother, and sister, the humble home, May-day, and Guy Fawkes's day. And yet there seemed no other way.

The father had no easy task to obtain a chance for his boy to learn a trade. What then could

be done with John? That question must have
occasioned anxiety in the Sandgate home, for
work he must, and to John's deep satisfaction it
was answered by a proposed trip to America and
a life there. A family about to move to America
agreed for ten guineas to add him to their circle,
secure a trade for him, and look after him until
he was of age.

America! O, how it thrilled a young boy's
heart! That was in 1829. Our country has
increased its attractions marvelously since then,
but it must have been a strong magnet even in
those days. An Irish girl, green as the isle she
hailed from, served in my family a while—fortunately for us, she served a little while. She
declared, before she came to America, that she
thought she could pick the "goold" off from the
trees! Deluded souls! The only fruit picked
by some has had a bitter taste, and far better
for such would it have been if they had stayed
in the old home amid the fields and friends of
childhood. However, America, fated to unmake
young Gough, was destined also to make him.
It was not easy for his parents to say good-bye.
When the London night-coach was rolling out
of the village by the sea John looked back from

his perch on the coach roof, and his eyes caught
glimpse of a wall near which waited and watched
a woman's lonely figure. It was the tearful
mother, who had gone ahead to steal one more
look at her boy.   He saw his parents again before
the ship was out on the Atlantic.   Off Sandgate
the wind died and the ship came to anchor.
People from the village put off to the ship in boats.
And who was it that rose in a little craft, the very
sight of him so cheering a home-sick boy?

"That's father!" was John's glad thought.
The old soldier was soon aboard, ardently kissing
his son.   Going to America then was a serious
undertaking, and as the sun dropped down the
western sky the boats from Sandgate fell off from
the ship, and then the visitors stood up and sang
—those on board joining—

> " Blest be the dear, uniting love
>   Which will not let us part;
> Our bodies may far hence remove,
>   We still are one in heart."

The song died away, the boats receded, lessened,
reached the shore again, and the night veiled
the sea with its shadows.   But who was it that
in the dead of night wanted to see once more the
emigrant boy?   It was his mother, accompanied

by his sister. They had coaxed a boatman—it took a half-guinea coax—to bring them to see once more the young emigrant, and when they left him he went to his berth to spend the rest of the night with his tears. When he went on deck again and looked about him the *Helen* was far at sea. Overhead the wind roared through the rigging. The great white sails, swollen by the breeze, were expanded like wings. Up and down, up and down, went the ship, breasting the long ocean swell, driving through the waters and throwing off the foam from her bows, while behind her the plowed ocean was white with her frothing furrow. Fifty-four days and nights of " up and down," only blue sea all around, only blue sky every-where above !

During that long voyage there was an abundance of time for thought, and John Gough profoundly thought. He wished—he was at home. He must have wished—he had been a different boy. He wished—but wishing was useless. Sometimes he would look through the scanty stock of possessions with which he was beginning life, and he would discover little slips on which were Bible passages. He well knew whose work this was. In his Bible verses also had been marked that he might pack them away in his memory. He knew who did the marking.

The sensitive, heart-sick boy thought of his home tenderly. It was of no avail. He was far at sea. Below the foggy horizon was Sandgate, away off in England. No going back now, only a going on and on, amid tumbling billows and under that ceaseless sky, blue and peaceful to-day, black with storm to-morrow. The 3d of August the *Helen* reached Sandy Hook. There was the New World just before the young pilgrim; and what did this ardent, sensitive, bright, fun-loving boy have with which to begin life on this side the waters? Twelve years, a small heap of clothing and other stores, at least four books, the Bible and Doddridge's *Rise and Progress of Religion in the Soul, The Economy of Human Life*, Todd's *Lectures to the Young;* a fund of old memories of the castle and its knights, of a soldier-father and his battles, of the adventurous Sandgaters and the big sea that defied them; a knack at recitation springing from his faculty of imitation and expression; a keen appreciation of the humorous in life; energy and ambition. Add to this a boy's inexperience and infirmities, and what may come of this venture in America?

CHAPTER IV.

A HOME ON A FARM.

TO a boy who had seen London, New York in 1829 could not have been a wonderful pict-ure. The family that John Gough accompanied expected to find a home on a farm in the State of New York. The first part of their journey was to go up Hudson River, and we will go with them. But take the map and trace that noble stream. Whenever you meet with a geograph-ical name not familiar to you, hunt it up. That you may be inclined to search out localities, have the atlas handy. Knowledge on a very high book-shelf, up where you cannot reach it, is likely to stay there. This Hudson River is fa-mous for its scenery. It possesses additional in-terest from the fact that its discovery was due to Hendrick Hudson, who, in the ripe month of September, 1609, found this river while hunting for China. As he did not know what water-course would take him to the land of tea-chests he concluded he might as well try the opening

we call New York Bay.   He followed the river
for a hundred and fifty miles, and came to the conclusion that no tea-chests could be found in that
direction.   He left this neighborhood when the
October leaves were turning gold and scarlet as
if to tempt him to stay longer.   It was Hudson who the next year discovered the big, cold
bay to the far north and now bearing his name,
and there on its blue waters his mutinous
crew set him and others adrift in a shallop
that receded, faded away, and was never seen
again.   Coming back to Hudson River we
would remember that on this bright stream
Robert Fulton, in 1807, successfully ran that
first steam-boat so astonishing the New World.
When that boat, the *Clermont*, went to Albany
it is not strange that spectators who saw this new
wonder at night described her as " a monster
moving on the waters, defying the winds and
tide, and breathing flames and smoke!"   It was
in a steam-boat that John Gough and his friends
went up the Hudson.   The vessel was doubtless
superior to the *Clermont*, but far inferior to the
steam craft shooting now between Albany and
New York.   John Gough had seen London and
the Atlantic Ocean, but he was not familiar with

such scenery as that turning the banks of the
Hudson into picture-galleries. He was delighted
with the views. The river-towns were very different from what they are now, but the river
was there and the hills were there. We can imagine this sharp-witted English boy looking with
admiring eyes at the Palisades rising up to an
altitude between three hundred and five hundred
feet. There were the beautiful bays Tappan and
Haverstraw. There were the heights of West
Point, where our government established its mil-
itary academy in 1802. Some young cadet on
the shore John may have seen from the deck of
his steam-boat and silently compared him with
the old veteran in Sandgate who used to put him
through the broomstick drill. Here in the High-
lands the young English pilgrim was deeply interested. We can see him running from bow to
stern, looking at this headland or that summit.
At Albany the steam-boat was left and the cars
taken? No car-wheels turning for his benefit
in 1829; but there is the canal-boat waiting
to carry the party on toward their home. They
are towed mile after mile, a big splash now and
then disturbing the quiet of their journey. The
noisy water meant their arrival at a lock by which

the canal-boat was shifted to a different level of
water.   It was a wonderful land that young
John, on the Hudson, had passed through, and
his quick eyes and keen ears did not permit any
new wonder along the canal to pass without a
challenge to show its mysteries.   The trip ended
at a farm in Oneida County, the English boy's
home for two years.   Here in his pilgrimage he
reached a corner in his life.   When God's pilgrim people had left Egypt they heard at Sinai
a trumpet-call to duty.

While young Gough was on this farm he heard
a call.   It sounded for him even as Sinai's trum-
pet was blown for Israel.   It was the voice of
conscience, and he obeyed the summons.   When
that summons may come there is only one course
to be taken; a refusal to hear is disobedience to
God and a harm to our most serious interests.
John Gough's obedience is no wonder.   He had
been brought up in an atmosphere of prayer at
home.   His mother had a religious nature pecul-
iarly susceptible.   The father was a Christian.
Their prayers came over the water for their
boy swifter than any white-sailed fleet that ever
sped across the Atlantic.   He was received on
probation into the Methodist Episcopal Church.

CHAPTER V.

ALONE IN NEW YORK.

FIFTY cents and a little trunk with which to conquer a position in New York! A seeker of his fortune stood at the foot of Cortlandt Street, his small trunk with him, poor, helpless, bewildered, not knowing what to do or where to go. He had just come down the Hudson River by steam-boat, and he was going—any body up in Canada or down in Mexico knew as well as he. What a very lonely place seems a crowded city to one who is a stranger, and this stranger now was a boy of fourteen, John Bartholomew Gough.

He had left the farm up in Oneida County. He did not feel satisfied with his situation there. During his stay of two years he had not gone to a school of any kind, during the week or on the Lord's day, and such absence from all fountains of supply was unsatisfactory to a boy thirsting to know more. For various reasons he felt inclined to make a change. He showed this good trait, a purpose to consult his father about learning a trade in New York before he left the country to hunt up an opportunity. He was poor, and postage in those days was more expensive than now. To raise the needed money to post the letter he sold a knife! I am wondering how long in those days of slow mails he waited before his answer came from England. His letter home reached Sandgate at last, and then an answer crawled back to Oneida County. His father told him to do as he thought best, and he now was at the foot of Cortlandt Street, New York before him, a diminutive trunk with him, and fifty cents in his pocket.

As he stood there staring about him, a man willing to earn a penny stepped up and asked where he would like to have his trunk taken. Where? Yes, where in the big city? New York was not as large as nowadays, but it contained about two hundred thousand people, a crowd big enough to swallow up this poor little pilgrim from the country and so effectually dispose of him that he would never be heard from again. But "where?" A cold wave of desolateness and loneliness swept over him. It chilled him to his very heart. But John Gough had not come alone to the city. He was like that patriarch of olden time who left home, kindred, country, but went out feeling that God was with him. Going into the world is ever serious. Ever take God with you. That blessed Bible verse came to him, "Trust in the Lord, and do good; so shalt thou dwell in the land, and verily thou shalt be fed." He was not so helpless after all. That old English grit that had traveled with him over the Atlantic came to his aid. Above all, the God of his English boyhood, the God to whom he had given himself amid the forests of America, strengthened him, and up to his shoulder went his trunk, and off moved Gough ready to go or do whatever Providence might suggest.

What would *you* do alone in a big city, entering it as a stranger, wanting to go somewhere and wanting to do something, but utterly at a loss as to place or pursuit? Put yourself in the place of that boy of fourteen. Get under his trunk. Make his situation your own. What would *you* have done? A boy not ashamed to carry his own trunk is not the most helpless being in the world, and if he will use his tongue and *ask*, and use his feet and *go*, he will find something to do and for it receive something to eat. Tongue and feet, readiness to ask, and

willingness to go—these are two essentials of success.   If a man come to me to sell something,
come as an agent for a book or some kind of
wares and I cannot trade with him, I am always
sorry not to give him my custom. We naturally
want to help one another. If he be bashful,
slow of tongue, not used to the business, and
without the energy which would naturally make
one qualification for the business, then I also pity
him. If he can talk, if he quit me only to hunt
up at once another customer, I say, "That man
does not need my pity. He will not be without
success." If you can talk, and if you will drive
round, never worry. You are sure to have some
measure of success.

Gough's first inquiry naturally was where he
could shelter his head. He went to a hotel
called the "Brown Jug." That was rather ominous when we remember the use to which some
brown jugs have been put. Gough did not hes-
itate to use his tongue, and, asking for work,
found an opportunity in the book-bindery of the
Methodist Book Concern. His pay per week
was two dollars and twenty-five cents. That
sounds small, but he found board for two dollars.
This enabled him to live inside of his income,

provided his clothes did not give out. It proved
to be a miserable refuge where he boarded. His
bed-fellow was an Irishman very ill with fever
and ague, and the bedroom was under the rafters
among the spiders. The second night Gough
had a bed—such as it was—to himself, but his
room-mate died in great agony of mind that very
night. Gough felt that his situation in New
York was any thing but agreeable. After the
above experience he was at his work trying to
labor patiently, but he wet with his big, hot
tears the paper he was handling. A young
woman saw him crying. She asked him the reason of it, and he was moved to tell her about his
life. "Poor distressed child!" she said; "you
shall go home with me to-night." When the
two reached her home, the young woman took
her mother aside, who soon came back and said,
"Poor boy! I will be a mother to you." The
lady was Mrs. Egbert, and she kept her word.

Poor boys away from home may thank God
heartily if they find in any one that sympathy
and counsel which made the old home bright and
strengthening. We may remember that Martin
Luther, when a needy student, used to sing in the
streets of Eisenach, hoping to receive for his

music a piece of bread.   One night, having been
turned away from three homes, he was making
up his mind to go to his quarters hungry and
faint.   He stopped to think about it before a
house in St. George's Square, and he asked himself if he must give up his studies, because so
poor and hungry.   Must he go back to his
father's home to work in the dark mines there
in the neighborhood?   While halting and debat-
ing, the door of the house before him swung
back, and Madame Ursula Cotta stood there.
She had previously noticed him at church services, and she now called him into the house, gave
him food, and became his friend.   It is such a
kind word that smooths many a rugged way,
and, perhaps, influences the course of a life-time.
Madame Cotta did not once think she was helping the glorious cause of the Reformation in
Germany meet and turn a hungry corner.
Young Gough found friends in New York, for
he put himself where he would be likely to find
friends.   A church in Allen Street received him
to its fellowship.   It is always an excellent plan,
especially if away from home, to place one's self
amid church associations.   It now seemed as if
a bright future were opening before young

THE METHODIST BOOK CONCERN, CROSBY STREET, NEW YORK.

Gough—but! How ominous is that word! How often we read of a life that runs off in uninterrupted prosperity, when abruptly that word "but" is seen in the narrative! It is like the train of cars gliding smoothly over a bridge until it comes to the open draw, and then suddenly there is a plunge downward. That "but" is the open draw.

I find no detailed explanation of the fact that young Gough forsook his church and his place of employment. He felt the influence of "circumstances," as he writes in that far-away, humble story of his life. Then he tells about temptation. He confesses carelessness in spiritual things. He had reached a "but" in his life. It did not probably seem so at the time, but in reality it was a serious change in his prospects. That old Book Concern on Crosby Street! Humble indeed its walls compared with those of the present palatial structure housing so many of the publication interests of the Methodist Episcopal Church to-day; but from the humble quarters on Crosby Street how far-reaching in many lives have been the streams of influence shooting off into the future! Many have been the private histories affected by the old house on Mulberry

Street. Gough's course might have been thus helpfully affected by his connection with that source of power. He neglected his opportunity. You can stand just here and see that John Gough is striking off into a course of shame and sorrow. He had come from the forests and the fields, from the pure atmosphere of the hills, from the clear crystal of the streams, into a Babylon, amid the distracting, confusing, tempting influences of the city, and it was soon to be seen that Babylon was too powerful for this impressible boy, sympathetic, social, quick to see, quick to hear, ready for laugh when others made the fun, and ready enough to make the fun for other people's laughter. He became careless in his religious duties. He drifted off into a life heedless of its obligations to God. Ah! when we virtually invite God to go out of our souls, who can tell what influences unbidden may come thronging in?

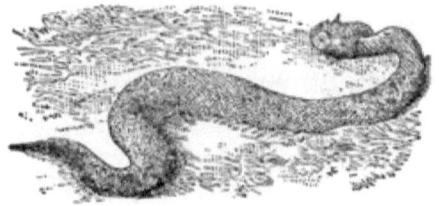

CHAPTER VI.

MOTHER IN AMERICA.

HOW great is the drawing of the heart toward the mother in a home! I can understand the feelings of the little girl who ventured to accept the invitation given her by an acquaintance to come into a strange cottage. The occupants were at dinner. Not a familiar face did she see within. She shrank from entering. When pressed to come forward she asked her friend in a child's simple way, "Is—there any —mother in there?"

"Yes, my dear, there is a mother here."

"O," she said, readily, "then I'll go in; for I'm not afraid if there's a mother there."

Is it any wonder that a homeless boy in America thought of the old home in England, that his love went fast and often across the waters, and that he wished mother could be with him? Couldn't father come too? And sister, if she were only with him! John's business was improving, and it seemed to him as if his

prospects would warrant the establishment of
the home-circle in America.   If he could only
get its links over the sea, that circle would at
once and hopefully be formed.   So he sent for
the links.   One Saturday afternoon in August,
when he was sixteen, a short message came to
him that threw him into great excitement.   It
was his own mother's handwriting saying that
she and her daughter were on board a packet,
and she wanted John to come to them as soon
as the ship was docked !   Yes, there was his
mother's handwriting !   There was her name !
That very moment the ship might be at her
moorings !   New York had at least one happy
boy that Saturday afternoon.   Down went the
work, and off went the worker.   Mother come
from England !   How the thought set his heart
to beating !   As he was tripping away, his shoe
needed mending, and he turned into a store
where he had told his mother and sister to call
when they came.   There he learned that his
mother had already called.   After he left, who
was it he saw hurrying along, apparently hunting up some address, glancing at a bit of paper
in the hand and then at the houses ?   It was a
little woman.

"Mother!" thought John.

Would she know this important American citizen now aged sixteen? He passed her, and then came back and repassed her. Greatness was not recognized. John could not wait any longer. He stepped up; he called, "Mother!" She turned, and what a hug she gave her boy! In the sight, too, of all New York—at least that fraction of it just then in that neighborhood. When he reached the barge where her luggage was he had another hug, and this time from his sister Mary, who sprang for him. John's father had not come. His pension from government detained the old soldier in England, and he hoped by waiting that he might turn it into cash in hand.

Mother, John, and Mary! Three of the family links in America. I can see them going up the street, talking and laughing, John loaded with an unusual sense of importance now that he is the male protector of this company, its proud escort amid the attractions of America's greatest city. John was then earning three dollars a week. His mother had brought a few household goods from England, and housekeeping was started at once. Cups and saucers for

three at their first tea, and not a rich feast on
the other pieces of crockery; but it was a happy
gathering, and no voice that I hear is more enthusiastic than John's. To be sure, they had
only two rooms, but two homely rooms, if con-
tented hearts are there, will hold more happiness
than all the gilded palaces of ugly strife in the
world. The autumn was one of comfort until
bleak November winds began to blow, and then
the winds swept straight and hard into the
Gough quarters.

"Hard Times" lost John his situation. Sister Mollie parted with hers for the same reason.
There they were, out of employment. What
could be done? I can see them staring at one
another in anxious inquiry. There were the two
rooms they lived in, for which they paid a dollar
and a quarter a week. They could and did give
up one, and then they multiplied this room into
two when night came, and the multiplier
was a curtain strung across the apartment. So
at night they had as many rooms as before,
and their weekly rent was only fifty cents. If
sticks of wood and baskets of coal and bags of
flour could be multiplied as easily, and as the
figures go up in quantity they also go down in

price, how cheap would living be for poor people! Now and then John had a chance to work, but any such spasms of employment could not prevent poverty's pinch. The winter was cold. The winter was hungry. Where could the mutton be found for the broth that Mrs. Gough, then in feeble health, one day longed for? John looked about his hungry home and thought of his best coat. It would not make broth, but he could pawn it for food. It went to the pawnbroker's, and back to the home came food for the family. New York then was nearer to the country than it now is. Sometimes John would push off a mile or two and lug home any pieces of wood he could pick up in the road. That hungry winter, once when he saw his mother crying he questioned her. He learned that the home was foodless. No bread, but sharp, biting hunger. He could not stand his mother's tears. Out-doors he went, and down the street he strayed, hungry, perplexed, crying. What was the matter, a stranger asked.

"I'm hungry, and so is my mother," John told him.

"Well, I can't do much; but I'll get you a loaf," replied the stranger.

He bought and gave John a three-cent loaf. Only a three-cent loaf; but how welcome it was! John went home with a much lightened heart.

"See, mother!" we seem to hear him saying as he springs into the one room that is the home of poverty, and yet home. It is not a barrel of flour that has come, but just a loaf, a three-cent loaf.

And the mother, she is so affected that she takes up that treasure-casket, the Bible. She lays it on the feeble old table of pine. She opens it. She reads from it, and then they all fall upon their knees, and she pours out her soul to God and beseeches the God of the poor to bless that humble loaf. Sweeter than all the bread of sin that John Gough afterward ate was that poor little lump of food up in the city attic, costing only three cents. I wonder if we realize how many people are glad to get just a three-cent loaf.

CHAPTER VII.

MOTHER GONE.

SPRING is apt to rout Hard Times. It brought relief to John and Mary Gough. They found work again. The coat that had traveled to the pawn-broker's journeyed back again to its nail in the garret. The summer, though, was a worse foe to John than the winter. His mother complained of weakness. Up in that garret with its one little window she felt oppressively the heat that poured down upon the roof.

One July day John wished to go off and take a bath. The weather was sultry, and his mother had been speaking of weakness, but it did not alarm John. He went away, first asking the favor of a lunch of rice and milk when he returned. Somehow that day John Gough was in special glee. With his friends on this bathing-trip he sang songs and joined in their careless laughter. He did not anticipate any serious trouble. He went home from that trip whistling away, careless as a bird at its morning song, and was passing

up the steps, when on the threshold of the door
of his home Mary met him. She grasped him and
said just these words: "John, mother's dead!"

What? It could not be! Mother dead?
If the sister had been an assassin and had dealt
him a heavy blow he could not have been more
overwhelmed with surprise. In a daze he halted.
He lingered, still bewildered. When he was
allowed to go up to his attic home there in the
awful hush of that secluded spot lay his dear,
dead mother! She had been found dead by a
young man who, passing the open door, saw her
prostrate on the floor, smitten down with apo-
plexy. There, among the relics of a fire in the
grate, subsequently was found the saucepan in
which she faithfully had placed John's rice
and milk, only a charred mass now on the bottom of the pan. What a pathetic relic! All
through the night he watched by that silent form
of his beloved mother. It was a night-watch of
pain, in long, long solitude. When the morning light broke gently in the east, and stole
through the one little window into that room
where the dead slept in peace and the watcher
waited in agony, John laid by her side the hand
he had taken in his, a hand that had toiled so

unwearyingly for him, but powerless now forever. Then he stole out into the city. It was a
world of unreality, and he was an unreal being in
it. He went to a wharf and there sat vacantly,
sorrowfully staring at the water. Mother dead!
Bewildered, burdened, he returned to what was
no longer a home. The coroner had been there
and left word about the burial and when it would
be. Burial? Where? How? Who had money
to pay for the interment? Again John went
out in his bewilderment and helplessness. Again
he was a confused wanderer. When he returned his sister told him about the people who
had been there. Laying his mother's body in a
box of pine they had carried it off in a cart to
the place of burial. John told his sister they
would follow the hearse. They must see the
burial. It was a humble train stealing to the
pauper's burial. In the street went the hearse
and its sad, silent load. Those who followed to
mourn were just that son and daughter, only
two to lament her, two that sobbed and went all
alone. At the burial-place one other coffin was
seen in the cart, and that was a tiny pauper, a little
child. There was no prayer over the mother's
coffin that was placed in a trench, earth commit-

ted to earth, ashes to ashes, dust to dust. The
two mourners watched the burial, and then in
sorrow moved away from the pauper's grave.

"Now, Mary, what shall we do?" was the
question that John asked his sister when they
came back to their poor, desolated home.

What next?

Death may come into our homes, but we cannot long seclude ourselves in the privacy of our
sorrow. Life presses hard upon death, and forces
its imperative duties upon our notice.

What next?

It was a very serious question.

The night of that day John could not endure
a stay in the home now so unreal, and he went
out into the darkness to wander about the streets.
Food was repulsive to him, and sleep seemed to
flee from him. That was recorded of the first
night.

What next? What in after days?

The old home was broken up. Sickness followed John Gough's vigils and his abstinence
from food. When he was recovering from it
he went among his old acquaintances, the Eg-
berts, who cared for him in his convalescence,
and then he visited his friends on the farm up

in the country. His sister found work in New York, and boarded in that quarter of the city where she was employed. John Gough was approaching a very serious epoch in his life. He had gone down into the depths of a terrible sorrow. His mother had thrown about him the restraining influences of prayer and the Bible. She was now dead. It was like lifting the smile of heaven off from the earth, taking away the sunshine, the light, the beauty and fragrance of blossoms, the music of birds. With such an atmosphere of summer that praying mother had surrounded her boy. What would he do without her? When he came back to New York he who had gone into this dark, terrible sorrow, must meet the world and all its distracting influences. How would he meet them?

Some day you go down into a gloomy mine. You descend by a pathway hollowed out in the sides of the abyss. At one side of that pathway runs a rope all the way down. As you descend, you count little niches, each holding a light, and what if these illuminate little placards saying, "Hold on to the rope!" Would you neglect those injunctions? You come to a place shrouded in darkness. You hear far, far below you the sound of a falling rock, the blow echoing up to you through those dreary spaces. How deep is that abyss! Would you not grasp that rope tightly? You reach another lighted injunction calling out to you, "Hold on to the rope!" Here the path has become very narrow. A careless step might send you abruptly down, down, into those awful depths. How you would cling just there! John Gough was going down into an abyss worse than the depths of his dark sorrow for his mother. He was to meet again the temptations, the perilous seductions of a great city. O, if he had only clung to prayer, that rope let down from heaven and holding us back from every precipice we may meet! O, if he had only clung to those other ropes of safety, the Bible, the society of Christian men and women, the Church of God! Let us hold on to every rope, and though temptations be not far away, they will not bewilder and attract us from the path. Between us and them is that *rope* of safety which God's hand itself has stretched for our guidance and support. Some young men never feel the temptations of city life, for they are careful to hold on to God's appointed helps for our souls. Let us cling to the rope!

CHAPTER VIII.

GOING DOWN.

IN the autumn after his mother's death John Gough, then seventeen years old, again went to work in New York. And he went among— tempters. What kind of tempters? Old topers from the dram-shops, with their red noses and pimpled faces, men who reeled at him out of the gutters, bringing their rags and filth, men raving in the midst of delirium tremens, men with palsied hands and trembling feet, about to sink into the grave? These are not the tempters that have influence over a young fellow like John Gough. He went among a circle of young men known as "respectable," but still convivialists, who liked "a glass"—several of them—on a table, and then surrounded it with their chat and laughter, their jests and songs. Into such a circle John Gough ventured, a circle more dangerous than the depths of any dark mine, and there he tarried. If he had been a young Spartan he would have faced a different

display of the drink-habit. The Spartans are
reported to have forced slaves to drink to a
state of beastly intoxication that the youth of
Sparta might see how disgraceful was drunkenness, how serious might be its evils. John
Gough saw those beginning the downward walk
of sin and shame, and was affected differently.
This was in 1834. We shall appreciate Gough's
peril more fully if we consider that there was
not a strong public sentiment to help him to
abstain from drink, and how much there was, on
the other hand, to encourage him to make a fool
and a failure of himself! Once the use of intoxicating beverages was exceedingly common.
There were certain Scotch-Irish settlers who
arrived in one of our States in 1710. They
were very devoted to their denominational stand-
ard of belief, and devoted to something else also.
It was said of them that they "never gave up
a pint of doctrine or a pint of rum."

Was it a funeral? This is an account of a
minister's funeral in those far-off days, when
almost every body drank liquor :

"Every man who attended the funeral was
met at the door, and a glass of rum, poured from
a flask, was there offered him. Every woman

was met in the same manner, and a glass was poured for her. As it was a minister's funeral at least a hundred and fifty must have gathered, and a hundred and fifty glasses must have been offered. Not every glass was emptied, and some, probably, were not touched, though we would not have trusted the temperance principles of the greater part of the mourners. We do not know how large the glasses were, but it would seem as if sixty pints of rum would be needed to start such a funeral. When the service was over, when the coffin had been carried to the grave, when the procession had come back to the house, then two rooms were set apart for a friendly glass. The bearers took one room and the people in general sat down in the other. In each room was a table, and this was decorated with bottles of rum, with tobacco and pipes. There the men tipped the bottles and smoked the pipes. How many pints, quarts, gallons of rum it took to close up the occasion 'decently and in order' I cannot say. It was said that one or two were drunk out-doors, and celebrated by singing funeral songs!" Well for society was it that only occasional were these minister-funerals!

Was there a religious gathering ? Dr. Lyman
Beecher, the father of Rev. Henry Ward Beecher,
gave this account : " At the ordination at Ply-
mouth the preparation for our creature-comforts,
in the sitting-room of Mr. Heart's house, besides
food, was a broad sideboard covered with decan-
ters and bottles and sugar and pitchers of water.
There we found all the various kinds of liquors
then in vogue. The drinking was apparently
universal. This preparation was made by the
society as a matter of course. When the consociation arrived they always took something to
drink round ; also before public services, and
always on their return. As they could not all
drink at once they were obliged to stand and
wait, as people do when they go to mill. There
was a decanter of spirits also on the dinner-table
to help digestion, and gentlemen partook of it
through the afternoon and evening as they felt
the need, some more, some less ; and the sideboard, with the spilling of water and sugar and
liquor, looked and smelled like the bar of a very
active grog-shop. None of the consociation
were drunk, but that there was not, at times, a
considerable amount of exhilaration I cannot af-
firm."

If at occasions professedly religious drinking was so common, how must it have been when men met just to work, to celebrate a marriage, or get mad over politics? At an election dinner over which the General Court of Massachusetts, in 1769, made merry, I find that this quantity of drink was necessary to stimulate those grave legislators to gleefulness and to wash down two hundred and four dinners, namely, seventy-two bottles of Madeira, twenty-eight of Lisbon, ten of claret, seventeen of port, eighteen of porter, fifty "double bowls" of punch, each containing two quarts, and also cider! The amount of the latter is not given, and it was probably stronger than sweet cider.

God did not purpose that the conscience of the Church should stay drowsy on this subject. In the last century there was some awakening of interest in the subject of abstinence. Still, there was a general apathy. In the present century there has been a very positive stirring of the consciences of men.

In 1825 Dr. Lyman Beecher, who was a famous pulpit thunderer, fired off six batteries against intemperance, and the six batteries were six sermons. Their echoes rumbled through and

startled New England. The ministers drove
liquor from tables at ordinations and in their
homes. In Boston, 1826, the American Temperance Society was formed " to restrain and prevent the intemperate use of intoxicating liquors."
In 1829 the New York State Temperance Society was started. It soon had a thousand local
societies and a hundred thousand members.
Then there was a wonderful movement called
the " Washingtonian." Its origin shows out of
what strange seed God's harvests may grow.
At a Baltimore tavern a drinking-club used to
meet. A temperance lecture was to be given in
one of the churches. What a good idea it would
be to appoint a committee to visit the church
and hear the lecture, and then to report to the
club! It is thought the motive in all this may
have been simply fun. However, the committee did their duty, heard the lecture, and brought
back a report. Then broke out a discussion. It
raged like flames in a hay-stack. When the land-
lord stepped in it was like another armful of hay
on the fire. Cold water may be good for fire, and
the flames spread when six pledged themselves
to total abstinence, starting a society. The name
chosen was the Washingtonian Total Abstinence

Society, and the year was 1840, the month April. From that center of activity went out a mighty influence. One John H. W. Hawkins, a poor drunkard, joined the society and became a cold-water champion. This movement is still felt.

It should be noticed right here that all this was in John B. Gough's young manhood, and not so early as the date when he joined his gentlemanly tempters in New York. The Washingtonian reform was half a dozen years away when John B. Gough ventured into the above circle of associates. Circle? It was a whirlpool of death, a maelstrom! Those friends were glad to see him. Bright, social, a fun-lover, a good singer, his memory packed with entertaining stories, and having such powers of imitation that he could easily act out each character in the stories, the young convivialists had a welcome for him. Where the foolish and wrong elements are so continuously cultivated the good must wither through neglect. His mother's wisdom was not repeated in the son's life. In his bramble-garden he had no place for such healthy growth as the precepts of that mother. Gough's talent for mimicry and gift at story-telling continued to make him popular, and, as an amateur, he tried his luck on the stage. His employer moving his business to Bristol, R. I., Gough followed him. He was in his twentieth year when his employer failed, and Gough went to Providence. He took his drinking habits with him, even as a prisoner carries round the chain and ball attached to his feet. He found work, and found also a chance to go on the stage. Finally he and his employer separated, and the mechanic became stage-actor solely. It seemed as if he were gaining notoriety by his performances when all these glowing promises of success came to a sudden end, like a rocket's fire. The theater shut up. Gough was not paid. The streets of Providence had another case of want.

He had, in one sense, less money, and yet drank more liquor—a feat to which only a drunkard is equal. One night he was so near pauperage that he kept moving about the streets almost until morning just to keep some measure of comfort in his body. To one of the city's lowest inns he went in his despair, and there found a shabby shelter. Work he had tried to get, but could not secure it. At last he was introduced to a man hunting up actors for a theater in Boston, and Gough was taken to that city and be-

came an actor there. The theater collapsed, and
Gough's pay collapsed with it. He was adrift
again, shabby, in want, with an appetite slowly
consuming him. He went to work again, but
January, 1838, he was out of work again. And
what was the reason assigned for the discharge
of this young man, not yet twenty-one? Too
shabby for his employer's place of work, and—
he drank!

Did not Gough understand his peril? He
speaks in after years of his susceptibility to the
poison in intoxicating drinks. He ought to have
appreciated it at this stage of his life.

Why did he not let drink alone? Ask the
slave why he does not break his hard, heavy
chains? "Can't," he says, pitifully. "Can!"
however, says the drink-slave. Yes, in theory.
He has the power, but he will not use it, and the
effect is the same when you will not as when
you cannot. The drinker continues to yield to
the seductions of drink. All the time it winds its
chains closer and closer about him, chains that
are heavier and heavier. At last, when he thinks
of throwing them off, he feels that he is chafed
and held by fetters whose strength is a surprise
to him. But where all this time was John

Gough's past? Where was the influence of home, of the mother that had followed him across the wide-rolling water, and in the spirit of a true consecration staying with him until her death?

Had he forgotten all this? Did he think of her at all? A cherished memory would have been a strong restraint. Sir Francis Phillips was accustomed to assert, "I should have been an infidel were it not for the recollection when my departed mother used to take my little hand in hers and make me say my prayers on my bended knees." Was there no thought of the past to hold Gough back from sin? If his mother had lived and he could have seen her daily looking at him, face to face, watching him, I cannot think he would have strayed so far. Visible presence is sometimes very powerful in its influence. General Swift, of Boston, once spoke of a habit that his mother had. She would say to him, "I want to live long enough to see you come to your Lord and to your Saviour." Once after she had heard him in the delivery of an eloquent address during the civil war she remarked, "If I could see you stand there and talk for your Saviour I would ask nothing more." One day when he was serving

the State of Massachusetts in its Legislature there
was a bill on the liquor question before the
house. If not actually prohibitory it was one
restrictive in its application. Those who sent
General Swift to the Legislature were not in
favor of the bill, and they looked to him to
vote accordingly. He intended that his vote
should express their wishes. When the day
for action came, somebody besides his constitu-
ency was looking at him, and that was his
mother, up in the spectators' gallery. She was
there hoping the bill would succeed, desirous
that her son should help give it success. There
she was, watching him. He expected to vote
with the noes, but when about to say no he
chanced to look up to the gallery, and there was
his dear old mother, looking down! She saw him
even as he saw her. To the astonishment of all,
including the voter himself, his voice rang out
clear and decided, "Aye!" Those who have
heard him know what a robust, penetrating
voice he has. His mother's influence had carried the day, and she was not astonished at the
result. "My son," she said, "I had prayed the
Lord not to let you vote wrong, and I knew you
could not."

5

A mother's visible influence! If Gough's mother could have lived on earth even as she lived in heaven, and could have brought her influence to bear upon him before the drink-chains once so soft and plastic had hardened and grown rigid, his life might have been very different. As it was, what outlook of encouragement was there for him ?

CHAPTER IX.

DOWN DEEPER.

NEWBURYPORT, Mass., is a charming old
sea-port town. Past it murmurs the bright
Merrimac, with its hushed songs of the blue hills,
crystal lakes, and green forests, which it has seen
and out of whose heart it has rippled and so
come singing down to the sea. The place is one
of varied business interests. The country people
come here to trade, manufacturers here drive
their busy wheels, and at its wharves the vessels
lift their wings and out of the river silently glide.

One winter evening, years ago, there came
from Boston to this interesting old town a young
man. He was not yet twenty-one. He was a
person of versatile talents. He could put a neat
coat on the back of a volume. He could tell and
act out effectively a good story. He could sing.
He had a power over others when he wished to
exert it in appeal that he himself little appreciated. Others felt it but did not adequately rate
it. Social, liking his kind, he might have become

the center of an ever-widening circle of influence
for good.   A new man even in an old town has a
peculiar opportunity, and this young book-binder
had it in this ancient town by the sea.   What a
power he might have here become!   He had
made his mistakes in the past, but he was not
obliged to repeat them.   What would John
Gough, the book-binder, do with his new opportunity?   He had come from Boston to improve
a business chance that had been reported to him.
He was to try the world again, on six dollars a
week.   Had he brought his old enemies with
him?   Would he leave the bottle behind?   He
did quit that, and he began life as an abstainer.
While he left the bottle behind, he had brought
with him the old social instinct, and he could
not very well come without it.   Unfortunately,
he decided to gratify it in the wrong direction.
If that social instinct had carried him where the
best influences were—and Newburyport had an
abundance of them—if he had gratified it in
church circles, it would have been a safe treatment.
For a few weeks he went without touching liquor.
It took a hard fight to do this, but while fighting
the enemy on the side of his appetite he surren-
dered on the side of his sympathetic, social nature.

He soon joined a fire-engine company. This kind of organization has always been effective in meeting fire and in fighting it with water, but before that combination, "fire-water," engine companies in the past have not always been victorious. Customs, though, have happily changed:

At Newburyport the bottle finally became Gough's companion, and the impression he made on Newburyport was far from favorable. In the summer, as work was scanty, the book-binder became fisherman. He went off on a cruise to the Bay of Chaleurs. The fisherman's life was rough, but as liquor could not easily be obtained the trip had its compensations. When on shore Gough made up for deficiencies, as he considered them, and drank deeply. Sometimes in visiting a vessel he could obtain the beverage.

A tippler is sure to do something foolish, if not fatal, when he ventures on the water. I once heard of two men who had been on a small trip by boat to a town, and at night started to go home. They knew enough to find their boat at a wharf, and knew enough to get into it, and knew altogether too much for their own good when they put a jug into the boat. They took up their oars and began to row. I can

imagine that they varied their pull on the oars
with a pull at the jug. But somehow they did
not make so much progress in pulling on their
oars as they undoubtedly did when trying to empty
their jug. Bewildered, confused, wondering what
obstacle hindered them, they found they had forgotten—to untie the boat! Gough's adventure
was not only a drunkard's error but almost a
fatal one. He with others had visited a craft in
the vicinity of his vessel, and he came back so
intoxicated that he went where drunkards are
apt to go, down to the bottom of the boat. In
that position others failed to think of him, and
they prepared, when boarding their craft, to
take up the boat in the usual fashion. This
method was to slip a hook into the bow and then
pull the boat up. The hook was inserted and
the boat was coming up, bow first, but Gough
was going down, tumbling violently into the
stern. It was a wonder that the drunkard who
had gone to the bottom of the boat did not go
to the bottom of the sea. Aroused by the fall,
he shouted, and was saved from a near death.

Did I call Gough a drunkard? He did
not think he was such. The word "drunkard"
suggests a situation where hope has almost

departed; and what tippler likes to say that? Dr. Johnson has remarked that "the diminutive chains of habit are seldom heavy enough to be felt till they are too strong to be broken." Gough had not come to any such conclusion. It is not surprising that he was unconscious of his real peril. It is Archbishop Whately who has asserted very truthfully, "Habits are formed, not at one stroke, but gradually and insensibly, so that unless vigilant care be employed a great change may come over the character without being conscious of any."

Habit is making and unmaking us all the time. Look out for habits. Gough did, but he looked out for the wrong ones. Steadily he cherished the habit of drink. He was absent three and a half months on that fishing trip. The crew had one very serious experience, that of an awful storm which sent old seamen to their prayers and almost sent the vessel ashore. Gough was now twenty-one. That year he was married, and as he had saved money while absent on his fishing trip he was able to buy furniture and begin home-life once more. It seemed as if the new home and his marriage vows would have aroused within him an ambition and a purpose stronger than any love for drink. Doubtless Gough's lips trembled with the excitement of vows made to consecrate that home to the purest, holiest influences. It is the home-life that should go down to the strongest motives and lay hold of them, even as a man in building strives to touch a strong, rock foundation. I knew a man who had been behind the walls of a penal institution. He had also been behind the walls of a habit that may be a still stronger prison-hold, and rum was the jailer. He had been released from the former. The grace of God had come into his heart, and in that strength he went out also to fight a battle with appetite. He was successful. He was blessed in a business effort. He had been married, and his wife soon expected to come to the town where he was and join him. He wanted a home. A man of strong, sympathetic feelings, he longed for companionship and longed for a place that could be called by that endeared name, "home."

"I cannot live without some one to tell my troubles to," he declared. "May I never suffer what I now endure alone again!"

He could not afford an expensive home, but he must have something. He hired two rooms,

over which was a small attic. The furnishings
were very simple, but to him all this preparation
was of greater interest than a king's equipment
of a palace. The ex-convict was now a new
man, and like other men he expected to have a
home. His soul was thrilled with this expectation.

"And now," he said to himself, "I must
dedicate my home."

Why not? Other institutions are dedicated,
and why not the ex-convict's home? But how?
His old chaplain happened to call upon him,
and he said the chaplain must go and see
his home and that it must be dedicated. So in
the simply furnished room that was both bedroom and parlor, about nine by twelve, the two
sat down on two plain wooden chairs. A fold
of red cloth between the cheap curtain and the
panes had been drawn across the upper part of
one of the windows, and the warm, cheerful
tone given to the colors in the room as the sunshine fell on this inexpensive red lambrequin
augured well for the approaching dedication.

Knowing the man so well, I can imagine just
how he looked as the services went on. They
were opened with the singing of the hymn, "I

need Thee every hour." Poor fellow! He had
known what that meant, and now that he was
going to have a home the voicing of his need of
God's blessing was fervent as ever. The services went on. a warm, hopeful flush of color
brightening the humble room. When the hymn
was concluded, then he opened the old Bible
bought with his earnings as a convict and read
from it the seventh chapter of St. Matthew,
"Judge not, that ye be not judged." In it is
that assurance, "Ask, and it shall be given you."
In the closing portion is that vivid sketch of
shattering rain and sweeping floods out of
which rises the house founded upon a rock.
The man's soul was tremulous with emotion.

"O, my God," he exclaimed, "how I have
prayed for a home! And O how I have worked
for it! And now here I am. Thank God!
But, O God, I want it to be a good home. It
must not fail me. O, it must help me to stand!
And O, I want it to be founded on the Rock—
on the Rock! Yes, brother, on the solid Rock—
on Christ Jesus—so that when the rain descends
and the floods come and the winds blow—so
that when the dreadful storms come—they have
come upon me before, they will come again—so

that when the great storms of awful trouble come down upon it, my home will not be destroyed."

Was this the sermon of dedication? Tears ran down the cheeks of the man. His soul shook with agitation as he saw the storm coming, then driving upon his home, which rose up triumphantly. Did it not rest on a rock? After this "sermon" of dedication came prayer; then the singing of "Nearer, my God, to thee," and the services were concluded. The chaplain and his assistant now left and took the audience also with them. The key was turned in the lock of the humble door. The two rooms and the little attic and the plain furniture were left behind—a humble spot; and yet did not the blessing of God tarry there as really as when Solomon dedicated his great temple and the glory of the Lord came down in a cloud and filled all the house?

Would not such a spirit of dedication have been blessed to the bookbinder's home in Newburyport? Would his mother's God have failed Gough if there had been a looking up to him? It was a very serious corner in his life that he was turning; and would he turn it right?

Blessed the life where God is invoked to stand at every corner and by his grace effect a right turn. Gough's life, though, was away from God. When his intensely social nature asserted itself, turning away from the home he had established, he turned to an unworthy social circle whose influences did not help any inclination to be temperate. There came another fishing voyage, the vessel going out and coming back in safety. The soul of John Gough, though tossed on this life's waves, did not find a harbor of refuge; would such ever be sought? and if desired would there be persistency of effort to reach it?

CHAPTER X.

RAYS OF LIGHT, THEN DARKNESS.

NEWBURYPORT is a place of strong religious influences. It believes in churches.
On a retired street stands an old house of God,
surrounded by many venerable and cherished
associations. Outwardly it is a quaint piece of
architecture, with its two diminutive belfries.
I have officiated within its walls, and can imagine myself in its pulpit many years ago waiting
for the opening of the services. Glancing door-
ward I can see a young man entering the
church. His appearance at once interests me.
He is not nicely dressed. I think he must have
made a special effort to come to church. I
fancy his wife has mended any rents in his clothes
and nicely brushed them. He has a quick,
sharply glancing eye, and there is a kind of in-
telligent self-assertion to his air, as if he knew
that he could be somebody if he wished or had
a chance. At the same time there is a shy,
startled look, as if he were not accustomed every

Sunday to such surroundings, and thought some
old godless companion might perchance see
him and wonder why he were there.   It is John
B. Gough.   There has been an unusual stirring
of the sense of obligation within him, for some
reason, and he has come to church.   If he had
only clung to this rope of the church when going down amid the temptations of the city it
would have held him in safe places.   It will
hold any one of us.   It will make a vast difference in our lives whether or not we cultivate
church-going habits.   To be found in the house
of God each Sunday means to be found in the
place of blessing, where Christ's hand will touch
us in sympathy and his voice cheer us amid de-
pression and sorrow.   Better still is it not only
to be inside church walls, but to be a member of
Christ's great flock.

When Gough went to the old church the
Rev. Randolph Campbell was pastor.   He was
a man of very positive opinions, which he knew
how to heat up and then deliver with energy.
When Gough heard Mr. Campbell he listened
to some very straightforward preaching which
had singular success in finding a man's conscience and arousing it.   I am not surprised that

Gough for a while tried to do better. Mr. Campbell's warm heart went out toward Gough, and he welcomed the young man to his house. He appreciated Gough's powers, and told him he hoped he might yet win an education.

Those were days of hope in the old city. Good angels seemed to fold their wings above the young man; and stooping to him did they whisper words of encouragement? Rays of light were breaking out of a clouded sky. Ah! it was young Gough still, with the old gifts, bright, witty, enthusiastic, and yet—craving the stimulus of alcohol and fond of the social circle. The light faded out of the sky and the clouds thickened again. Good angels seemed to sigh and retreat heavenward. The better things awaking in Gough's nature went into an evil slumber again. His drinking habits were aggravated. Work ceased. Poverty pressed closer. Hunger was keener. That hunger and want, those thin, spectral visitants, should throw so thick and dense a shadow in the drunkard's home is no contradiction or wonder. In Manchester, England, a working-man was making a temperance speech. He held in his hands a knife and also a loaf of bread. Drawing the knife across the loaf and taking off a slice of moderate size, he said, "This is what you give to the city government." He made another and larger section, and added, "And this is what you give to the general government." He now made a tremendous slash with his knife that cut away a quantity of bread equal to three quarters of the entire loaf. "This," he said, "you give to the brewer." The remnant after all this amputation was only a thin slice. The larger fraction of this he allotted to the "public-house," and of the few crumbs left he said, "And this you keep to support yourself and your family." The drunkard's children knew this well. But Gough experienced something more cutting than hunger. People avoided him. Young men he had been the companion of, young men, too, who drank but could maintain a better appearance than he, gave him the cold shoulder. The singer in bar-rooms, the humorous story-teller, saw that his society was not desired now. He requested the company of a boy in a walk, and it was refused, the boy saying his father had warned him against Gough. It stung him to be neglected. It stung him to be virtually placarded "dangerous." To stop the smart he would drink. When he came to himself again he would soothe his pain with another deadly draught.

The light was vanishing. It seemed to come back when a rum-seller did an act of generosity you would not expect in one of that trade. No, it was an act of justice. This man helped Gough go into business on his own account. As Gough had helped support the rum-seller's bar, it was only just that the bar should help support Gough's bench. Gough might have prospered now, but the resources he was furnished with only made fuel for those fires that alcohol kindles. Gough, being master in his shop, could do as he pleased, and his pleasure was to neglect his business and gratify the craving for drink. He had one solemn warning. A young man whom Gough well knew begged for the loan of a coin common in the days of my boyhood, a ninepence. The money lent was turned into liquor, and the liquor was turned into the young man. The poor victim of rum begged a second piece of money. Gough denied him. While Gough was out of his shop, this devotee of the bottle swallowed a quantity of spirits of wine which Gough found useful in his work. Gough did

6

not see him again. Very soon after this he
heard that the young man was dead.

How did he treat this warning ? When Luther,
the great reformer, was in his earlier days perplexed about his future calling he was traveling amid the mountains. Storm-clouds gathered
and darkened above him. The thunder rumbled
and crashed in heavier and heavier discharges.
The lightning drew its awful sword of fire in.
the heavens. There came a blinding flash, and the
lightning smote down through the sky and buried
itself in the earth before Luther. He was overwhelmed with fear. He fell upon his knees.
Death seemed to confront him. Eternity
opened just there. In that supreme moment he
made a vow which brought to an end all his
indecision. If God would only shield him from
this peril he would forsake the world and set
himself entirely apart to God. Then he began
to question himself concerning his spiritual condition, and for a better life sharp now was his
craving. To carry out his new purpose he was
inflexibly resolved. He called together the old
school friends at Erfurth, where he had followed
learning's pleasant paths. He gave them a supper. There was music at the gathering. Wit

and mirth were there.   Suddenly, at the height of the joviality, Luther spoke and announced his purpose to give himself to the most serious of callings.   His gay companions were surprised. They strove to reason him out of his purpose. He was firm, however.   That very night, as if afraid that he might change his mind if he delayed, he stole away from his lodgings and alone went to the convent of the hermits of St. Augustine.   He knocked at the gate, and it opened, and into the convent passed the young man who, taught of the Spirit of God, was destined to become the great reformer.   He was at that time not twenty-two years old.   He met the warning of providence and accepted it. It is the only safe course we can follow.   It is the only course that we should pursue.

God   was   not   content   with   sending   plain warnings to Gough; there came an invitation. The wave of temperance reformation rolled to Newburyport one day, and a reformed drunkard spoke in the church of which Mr. Campbell was pastor.   The house was full.   But what old-young drunkard came with the crowd, with haggard face, with bleared eyes, and in his poor, threadbare clothing?   It was the book-binder, and the speaker's words went like a sharp sword into Gough's conscience. I do not wonder that he only stayed about ten minutes, but as he was passing out of the church a piece of paper almost tripped him up and stopped the drunkard in his course. It was the temperance pledge tendered Gough by a young man. A good impulse came to Gough as if it were the strong touch of an angel, and he did stop and was inclined to sign, when it would seem as if an evil angel came on the other side of Gough, and, as the craving for drink stirred within Gough, reminded him that he had a pint of brandy at home. Gough hesitated. Gough declined. Gough said, though, to himself, he would consume what liquor he had on hand and then— quit! That was like standing by a hay-mow in a barn, holding a card of matches in the hand and saying, "I will light these matches and touch them to the hay, and then have nothing more to do with matches in this barn." The wave of temperance interest coming to Newburyport did not trouble Gough to any serious extent. He was worse after this opportunity than before it, because he abused it. The lights of hope were now going out faster than ever.

CHAPTER XI.

IN STILL DARKER DEPTHS.

A DRUNKARD will practice deceit. Alcohol, that deranges the body, dislocates all the machinery of a man's moral nature. It may incline him to lie and to steal, and then it paralyzes the will-power that would prevent him from lying and stealing. It is like a train on a track where the switches are set wrong, and then some one ruins the brakes that would stop the moving train ere it makes the wrong turn. In Market Square, Newburyport, stood the old town-pump that, summer and winter, never refused a drink to the applicant who could move its handle. Its brimming trough was a good friend to dogs and horses slaking here their thirst. Be it the beggar in rags that swung up and down its handle, or the old tar just in from a voyage to the West Indies, or the parson in his well-brushed but seedy broadcloth, the town-pump never refused to bring up its cool, clear, crystal water when a muscular application was made at the handle. Gough thought it would be a good idea to swell the cold-water column. He did not want people to think he never drank any thing but rum. So he would come with his pitcher to the old town-pump. But is he not looking round to see if any body is near him? Glance into his pitcher. If an adept at such recognition you will see a pint of new rum in it! Clank, clank, clank, now goes the old squeaking handle, and down into the book-binder's pitcher falls a sparkling cascade, but there is never so much water as there is rum in the pitcher. Gough goes away, the drops of water, like globules of crystal, dripping from the outside of the pitcher. " Guess some folks will see that I use water as well as they," I fancy the book-binder is saying. If they could only have smelt the inside of that pitcher! He was sensitive to public opinion when sober, and defied it and despised it when drunk. That is the consistency of the drunkard's course. At Newburyport Gough sank lower and lower. His sister had married, and, living at Providence and prostrated by sickness, she sent for her brother's wife to help her. Gough, thus left to himself, felt his loneliness; but how did he meet his want of society? Whose companionship did he court? A gallon of West India rum, and finally another drunkard. What a shameful time they had, those three, the gallon of rum and the two drunkards! Gough's companion at last staggered home, and Gough was left alone with the balance of the rum. . For three days the drinking fit continued. One night terrible feelings attacked him. He wanted to sleep. His thirst being like a furnace, he tried to quench it with rum, and he sought also to stupefy himself into slumber. Baffled, he seized a tobacco-pipe and matches. He could not stand upright to kindle the latter, and, prostrate on the bed, he there scratched one against the wall and so lighted his pipe. He smoked and began to be drowsy. Aroused by a sensation of heat, he found that his pillow was burning! He unconsciously had set it on fire. He tossed it on the floor, and then fell back into a stupid slumber. When he awoke he saw neighbors in his room, who, attracted by the odor of the fire, had rushed in to learn the cause. They aroused him and lifted him from the bed, in whose straw was a smoldering fire! A while longer, and he might have become a cinder. The

accident shocked him, and still—he drank. A
horrible agony followed. He sent for the doctor. When the physician came the drunkard did
not want to meet him, but he could not avoid
the doctor, who ordered Gough's friends to
watch the drunkard and deny him liquor.

The "horrors," in English, "*delirium tremens*," in Latin, but in both languages an awful
penalty for sin, now set in. Gough was at the
bottom of those depths down through which he
had been plunging. Do we understand what is
meant by this awful and penal visitation?
Gough, in later years, in an anniversary address,*
May 6, 1875, before the National Temperance
Society, relates this case : " A gentleman said to
me last winter, ' It seems hard that drink should
come into my house when I have been fighting
it. I have a family of six children, four daugh-
ters being married. My youngest son is twenty-
six years of age ; he has had *delirium tremens*
twice, and is dying.' The physician, who related
to me many of the circumstances of the case,
sat by his side and said to him, ' Charley, you
know me and know that I am your friend. Now,

* *John B. Gough, His Anniversary Address*, p. 33, National
Temperance Society.

my dear fellow, you have a terrible time before you; you have to suffer intolerably for ten days or a fortnight. I think I can see my way clear to get you on your feet and save your life. If I get you on your feet and you touch liquor again, do not send for me.' The young man looked in his face and said, 'Doctor, you say I have to suffer. What do you know about it? Doctor, it is coming on me! I can feel it coming! What do you know about it? You could describe it, I suppose. You could tell your class in a medical school all about it. You could tell them how you amputated a limb, but could you tell them how the man felt when the saw touched the marrow? Doctor, if you can prove to me there is no physical suffering in hell I will cut my throat, for there is no mental anguish to compare with what I know I have got to go through. Doctor, I have had great spiders draw their soft webs all over my face and in my mouth. I have had green flies buzz in my ears and crawl up my nostrils and creep across my eyelashes. Ah, keep them off, doctor!' Yes, 'it' was coming! O, it was that awful thing coming, the 'horrors' even, rushing at him! The narrator went on to say, 'In less than three

minutes two men were holding him down.'
When he got on his feet he was weak and worn
and wasted. He walked with two sticks, just
able to keep himself up. On the third day he
was out and went into a saloon exclaiming, 'Give
me a little brandy, just a tablespoonful, not
much. Don't tell any body any thing about it;
it will do me good.' The man gave it to him.
'And now,' said the father, 'that boy of mine is
dying.'"

Such was the outline of the experience of
one who knew what the fight with alcohol
was when it hurled at him all the agony of
the "horrors." Into that awful pit, that chasm
of darkness, peopled with snakes, dragons, tigers,
demons, Gough, not an old drunkard, but still a
young man, was now driven by the *delirium
tremens.* It was blinding fire and then awful
darkness. He seemed to be plunging down,
down, down, into fearful depths where demons
leered and frowned at him. Out of his contor-
tions he would come so weak, all vitality seem-
ingly gone, helplessly lying on his bed, as if he
had been thrown there after violent wrestlings
with a wild beast; and then would spring at him
the awful thought that these terrors would begin

again. When Gough crawled out of his den of
nightmares he thought of her who had been a
mother and a counselor to him. That praying
mother! What had he done with her counsels?
What a difference in his life it would have made
if he had always shown that regard for a mother's teachings displayed by a certain drummer-
boy! A favorite with the officers, he was invited
by the captain to take a glass of rum. He refused, alleging, "I am a cadet of temperance,
and do not taste strong drink."

"But you must take some now," urged the
captain. "You have been on duty all day, beating the drum and marching, and now you must
not refuse. I insist upon it."

The boy, though, was resolute and still declined.

"Our little drummer-boy is afraid to drink,"
remarked the captain. "He will never make a
soldier." This he said to the major.

"How is this?" said the major, jokingly.
"Do you refuse to obey the orders of your captain?"

"Sir," said the boy, "I have never refused to
obey the captain's orders, and have tried to do
my duty as a soldier faithfully; but I must re-

fuse to drink rum because I know it will do me an injury."

"Then," said the major, gravely, wishing to try the boy, "I command you to take a drink, and you know it is death to disobey orders."

The boy looked straight into the face of the officer, saying, "Sir, my father died a drunkard, and when I entered the army I promised my dear mother that I would not take a drop of rum, and I mean to keep my promise. I am sorry to disobey orders, sir ; but I would rather suffer any thing than disgrace my mother and break my temperance pledge."

Could any thing be said after that by major or major-general even ? The boy's course was approved by his officers, and he was encouraged to be steadfast.

John Gough could not forget his mother's counsels. In moments of heart-searching he plainly saw his sin and earnestly determined he would do better. For a month he lived away from the rum-bottle. What a sign of his ability to do a grand work for himself all this seemed ! The next experience, what a sign of his inability to do this work in his own strength ! His wife . came home. In his happiness at her return, thinking that Gough was master and Rum was servant, he indulged in a glass of brandy. It was the first impulse again toward the bottom of the precipice up which he had painfully climbed. After the first glass came the second, and then another, and he went to sleep that night of his wife's return—drunk. He was again at his cups.

The intemperate book-binder had his seasons of reform. Does one ask why he did not succeed? A reformed man gave this testimony: "I never went to bed sober for ten years. The paper on which I've written down the words 'I'll quit drink' would cover all that side of this large hall. But there was One who could help me not to drink, and who can help every man—just one—the Lord Jesus Christ."

That testimony is corroborated by this fact: A drinking man, one confirmed in the habit, was about to go off on a fishing cruise. He suggested to another fisherman that before leaving they should "take a drink."

"No," was the answer, "I don't drink."

"Don't you drink any thing?"

"No, I don't drink any thing."

"Why not?"

"Because I am a Christian."

" What ! " asked the first man. " Does Christ keep you from drinking ? "

" Yes, Christ keeps me from drinking."

These words made a deep impression on the mind of the drunkard. He said to himself, " There is help that I didn't think of." Going home, reaching his room, kneeling down, he pleaded, " O, Lord Jesus Christ, keep me from drinking ! " Above him was a divine face tenderly looking down, and around him was thrown a divine arm that held him up and kept him from drinking. When would Gough look up to that pitying face and lean on that strengthening arm ?

The book-binder was now to become something else. He changed his plans for daily work. He had several times during his Newburyport life sung at concerts in different towns, and he now engaged to assist in showing the public how the battle of Bunker Hill was fought. It was a very peaceful kind of fighting called a diorama. Gough traveled about with these show-heroes of Bunker Hill. His employer retained him, though Gough persisted in lugging along the bottle for a companion. Finally Worcester was reached, that beautiful inland city of

Massachusetts, destined to play a very important part in Gough's life. It was October. The hills and valleys were brilliant with color, as if England's scarlet-coats at Bunker Hill were marching up and down the country maneuvering for another battle. Gough determined he would quit drinking. He resolved also to send for his wife, that long-suffering woman, and he inclosed in his letter his purpose to begin a temperate life. The evening she reached Worcester, when he met her, he showed her how well he could keep his promise ; he met her—drunk !

Gough soon left the heroes of Bunker Hill and obtained work and—still drank. His employers were told that he had been off on a spree, and they threatened to discharge him. His wife was now sick, and her sickness and that threat sobered him. Again he said he would reform and —did not. His wife's sickness became very serious. Still he drank. His wife and child that had been given him both died. Still he drank. He was in an awful world. Smitten with a sharp sense of loneliness, yet drinking while the dead lay under his roof! In the gloom of the night he would creep to those silent ones. In his despairing solitude his trembling hand

would touch those still faces, and then, going
back to his couch, he would lift the poisoning bottle to his lips.   After the funeral services shame
and despair were more intense.   Society spurned
him.   Work he had, but it was under restric-
tions.   He felt galled, crushed, hopeless.   Still
he drank.   He would have liquor.   He owned
various books and a few souvenirs.   These he
sold for rum.   What will a man not part with
that he may obtain rum?   To get it, what meth-
ods he may resort to!   Under the influence of
it, to what deeds he may be solicited!   In the
East they tell of a man who was met by one of
the genii, a fabulous class of beings more powerful than men, and the choice of three evils
was given him.   He could commit murder, he
could steal, he could get drunk.   The man naturally did not wish to be guilty of crime.   He
thought he would submit to the least evil—he
would get drunk.   When he was intoxicated,
though, the drunken fool both stole and mur-
dered !

When various sources of rum-supply failed
Gough he did this.   There was his old knack at
story-telling ; there were his powers of mimicry ;
there was his gift of song.   He would turn into

some despicable grog shop and there sing a humorous song or tell stories or in some other way use his power to entertain, and the boisterous, applauding auditors would pay him in drink.

Conscience, though, was not dead. Affection had not ceased to throb in his bosom. In the midst of the maudlin shouts of the grog-shop he would see his mother as she tried to win him out of these chains. Hour after hour, in the darkness of the night, did he lie on his wife's grave. Haunted by unhappy memories, pursued by a guilty conscience, driven by the horrible desire for liquor, without home, without friends, it is no wonder that once he went to the railroad track, a bottle of laudanum his companion, meditating suicide. The stupefying poison had reached his lips when he stopped. It was that pause which saved him. Gough was not the only one who has visited the railroad track purposing self-destruction. A poor fellow was found dead one day, terribly mangled, on the track of one of our railroads. He had deliberately selected a spot in a twist of the iron road where the engineer could not detect him until it was too late to stay his purpose. Prostrate he

7

awaited death, and it came, driving, roaring, crushing. Among his clothes was found a confession which he had prepared. He told why he had selected that spot, saying he could not be seen until it was "too late to stop the engine. Thus I shall go out of the world with a rush. I have fortified myself with some forty-rod whisky which I got at the Hollow, where may be found more of the same sort. Whoever finds my dead body and this paper, will know who I am. Send my personal effects to my wife, Mrs. —— ——, in ——. I did this by my own hand. Rum is the cause. I have but one regret ; that is my wife, for she has been a wife to me in every sense of the word. But I cannot live any longer, for I am tired of life. So, now, farewell to the world." There followed other words, and among them was a reference to a brother : " I hope he will shed one tear in memory, and then let me be forgotten !" He closed with this pitiful outcry : " Father, I wish I could live to fulfill your hopes and wishes, but I cannot ! O, rum, rum, rum !"

What influence kept Gough from suicide as he stood by the railroad track ? Did some good angel lay a restraining hand on his arm when he raised that bottle of benumbing poison to his lips? I know that angels do minister to the needy of earth. Gough turned away from that selected place of death, but what would he do? If he did not die under the wheels of the locomotive, he seemed to be fated to perish before that pitiless demon drink.

The last Sunday of October has come. How chilly are the streets of Worcester! The sharp evening wind rustles and sweeps aside the dead leaves of autumn. A drunkard, who feels the sting of the wind, comes sauntering along. He has been drinking and is under the influence of liquor still, but he is not insensible to a kind word or a cross one that may be spoken. He can appreciate a touch of sympathy or a rough hand of restraint. He feels his loneliness, for he is without a home. He feels his uselessness in life, for he is without any serious purpose. He shrugs his shoulders, for cutting is the wind and his clothing is scanty and shabby. It is not any despondency of old age that burdens him. He is young and yet nigh unto despair, for he is a drunkard. As you look, you can see through the shadows that gloomy face. You can hear the uncertain, uneven walk of this drunkard.

This very night John Bartholomew Gough is to come under the influence of a movement destined to revolutionize his life. What will be its character?

October! It is not a month when the gardener looks for hopeful beginnings. It is harvest-time, not seed-time.

A drunkard's life! It offers to the eye but little hope. God, though, reigns.

CHAPTER XII.

A FRIENDLY HAND.

YES, what will be the nature of this revolutionary influence in Gough's life? He is to be stopped in his career. Shall he feel a hand of violence or that of kindness and sympathy?

Some men cease to become drunkards when they become convicts. It may, in one way, be a great blessing to a man when he steps into the shadow of such a shame as imprisonment. A physician was asked by a man if he could cure a malady of his eyes. "Yes," said the doctor, "if you will follow my prescription." "O, certainly, doctor," said the patient. "I will do any thing to have my eyes cured. What is your remedy, doctor?" "You must steal a horse," said the doctor, gravely. "Steal a horse, doctor?" cried the astonished patient. "How will that cure my eyes?" "You will be sent to the State prison for five years, where you cannot get whisky, and during your incarceration your eyes would get well," was the physician's answer.

The man with the sick eyes tested not the worth of this prescription, but if he had it would have been a sure cure. Is Gough to try what strong walls can do for him ? As you watch him staggering along the sidewalk, is an officer to spring upon him, handcuff him if need be, and carry him off to the lock-up ? There is another influence besides that of rough hands which will restrain men.

There was an old drunkard known as " Bill Strong." Who ever thought that " Bill Strong" could be saved ? Somebody, though, had that opinion. One morning the barkeeper whom Bill Strong patronized led forward a lady, and, pointing at the old drunkard seated at a pine-table, said, " That's Bill Strong, ma'am," and left the two together.

" Am I rightly informed ? Do I address Mr. William Strong ?" she asked, in a sweet tone of voice, glancing pityingly at the drunkard's face. Mr. William Strong ! Was that the man's name ? He was not used to it, and yet it pleased him to hear this title of a respected manhood applied to him.

" Yes, that is my name, ma'am," replied the drunkard, stealing a look at his clothing, which needed rejuvenating. He even attempted to cover up a ruptured elbow of his coat.

"I am very glad to meet you, Mr. Strong," said the lady. "I have heard my father speak of you so often, and of the days when you and he were boys together, that I almost feel as if we were old acquaintances."

She continued the conversation. And what came of this interview? There was a certain document which she offered, and he attached his name. "Bill Strong?" No, but "William Strong," under the temperance pledge. It was the friendly hand that reached the old drunkard.

That was to be God's method for reaching Gough—a friendly hand. That bleak October night, when he was stumbling along without home or hope, he felt a pressure on his shoulder. Startled, he turned and looked at the person who had laid a hand on him. Instinctively he felt that it was the touch of a kind friend, for with the touch went a friendly voice. It was not the stern address of a policeman who has grasped a rogue. To this extent Gough had no difficulty in interpreting the meaning of this detention by a stranger that October night, chilling and lonely. But what else did the touch signify?

Gough was imagining what the stranger's errand might be.

"Mr. Gough, I believe?" said the man.

"That is my name," was the reply, and Gough would have left him.

"You have been drinking to-day."

This remark was a serious charge, and it might have provoked the person accused, but, oftentimes, it is not the thing said so much as the way it is said which does harm. This person's manner was very kindly.

"Yes, sir, I have," was Gough's frank reply.

"Why do you not sign the pledge?" asked the stranger.

Again Gough gave a frank answer that he did not hope ever to be a sober man, that there was nobody who cared for him or what became of him, that he did not expect to live long, and he did not care how soon he died, whether also he was drunk at the time or sober. Gough was reckless, and plainly told his interlocutor so. The man was not to be discouraged. In a brotherly way he took the drunkard's arm and asked him how he would like to go back to his old antecedents, to be honored, suitably clothed, attending church, on the old footing among friends, a man that was of use in society?

" O," answered Gough, " I should like all these things first-rate, but I have no expectation that such a thing will ever happen. Such a change cannot be possible."

" Only sign our pledge," was the reply to Gough, " and I will warrant that it shall be so. Sign it and I will introduce you myself to good friends who will feel an interest in your welfare and take a pleasure in helping you to keep your good resolutions. Only, Mr. Gough, sign the pledge and all will be as I have said, aye, and more too."

It may seem singular, but the interest of Gough was greatly aroused. That which deepened Gough's interest was the stranger's kindness of manner, and was the future this man had painted an impossibility? Could Gough deny it?

He determined to make the effort.

" Well, I will sign it," was his answer.

" When?"

" I cannot do so to-night—"

He now added a strange reason, but it shows the contradiction between the impulses of the drunkard's appetite and the convictions of his better nature. "For I *must* have some more drink presently, but I certainly will to-morrow," added Gough.

Some people might have been so discouraged at this answer as to turn away in despair. What if a man on a raft drifting toward Niagara Falls, and urged by friends to leave it for a boat that will take him to the shore, should say, "I will just stay and give my raft a few more shoves toward the falls, and farther down the stream I will quit the raft?" The stranger was not discouraged. He held on to his man.

"We have a temperance meeting to-morrow evening," he said ; "will you sign it then ?"

"I will."

"That is right. I will be there to see you." As he spoke he seized Gough's hand.

"You shall," Gough assured his new friend.

As Gough turned away he reflected, "If it should be the last act of my life, I will perform my promise and sign it, even though I die in the attempt ; for that man has placed confidence in me, and on that account I love him."

Still, Gough must have his liquor first. He must drift still nearer the fatal cataract of drink before leaving the place of danger! Inside of half an hour he had put himself outside of four glasses of brandy quaffed at a vile rum-hole! He went home drunk, and on his bed was stupidly unconscious all that night. When he awoke, the very first recollection coming to him was that of his promise to become a temperance man. What had he done? He almost regretted the hasty step. Besides, the furnace in his body was crying for fuel. He felt so miserably that he concluded he must drink. He went out to a hotel and imbibed a quantity of " bitters." He passed to his customary duties, but he could not forget that promise about the pledge. What would he do? Appetite strengthened as the time drew near for its promised subjection. At noon he swallowed a glass of the liquor for which his body had so intense a craving, and yet he was going to the temperance meeting that night! He was resolved, as the dark deepened, to go and keep his promise. That night the rally was to be in the so-called lower Town Hall, Worcester. Let us go also and be on the lookout for the book-binder.

The people are coming in, of all ages except the very oldest and very youngest.

Under the old coats, under the worn shawls, and under coats and shawls not old and worn, how many hopes and fears have a lodging-place! In every temperance meeting how many anxious hearts are present! How many sad, serious misgivings there are! What if this one should not sign the pledge, or, if one has signed, what if there may have been a fall, and his place now be vacant? The meeting has begun. All faces are turned toward the person who presides. Where is Gough? You don't see him. Has he not come? There is no one present that you think is Gough. Can he have failed to keep his word? The meeting goes on. Who is that standing up to speak? He is a young man, but a sorry-looking one. His faded brown overcoat he has buttoned up to the chin, as if he wanted to hide his very poor clothes beneath. He is not used to this work of addressing temperance meetings. He is agitated and nervous. You infer that there is a good deal of trembling under that old brown coat. He has caught the eye of a man who is smiling at him, and it encourages him. This smiling face down in the audience looks like that of a man who stopped a poor drunkard in the street last night and asked

him, in a kind, sympathetic way, to quit drinking. We shall find out who it is. The speaker
goes on, much agitated and yet resolute to tell
his story. It is the old story of the ruin that
rum had wrought. He says he has promised to
sign the pledge and he will now proceed to do
it. His hand shakes. His letters are uneven,
but there is his name on the pledge. Look at
it—"John B. Gough!"

Sensitive he must have been as to his appearance and action, but he could not appreciate
these as another could. I find in a Worcester
paper* this statement:

"How well many remember that pale, haggard face, the long, flowing, unkempt hair of
raven blackness, which Gough nervously pushed
back from his forehead as he entered the meeting. His coat was buttoned at the top only. A
crowd of those who had laughed at his baccha-
nalian songs, his wonderful powers of mimicry,
and his grotesque dancing had followed him
into the meeting. As he nervously affixed his
signature to the pledge a half-suppressed, sneer-
ing laugh was heard by those in the rear of the
hall. Gough heard it also, and, as he laid down

* *Worcester Spy*, February 26, 1886.

the pen, he turned suddenly upon those assembled with, 'Why do you laugh? Am I not a man?'"

Those who heard his words that night long remembered them.

The manhood within him was aroused at last, breaking away from its chains and asserting itself.

People in that far-away temperance meeting, back in the history of a previous generation, were moved to tears. What an event, not simply in Gough's life, but in its relation to other lives! Thousands signed when that one man wrote down his name. Thousands began to drop their chains when he stooped to wrench off and throw away his fetters. Through that shabbily clad young speaker how many would be brought out of the bondage of rum into the glorious liberty of total abstinence!

There were friends of Gough who rejoiced over the stand he was taking. There in the audience was the man who had sent up to him a smile of recognition when he began to speak, the man who, the night before, had asked him to attend this meeting, Joel Stratton. What an evening of victory and joy it was for him!

I am thinking, too, of another friend, Gough's mother. Some good angel, singing all the way, must have flown skyward to carry home to that mother the tidings that "John" had signed the pledge.

But what a night for the son followed this step! His will but not his appetite had consented to that pledge-signature. Such a burning thirst as he took with him from his bed in the morning! He was determined, though, to be true to his promise. It was a hard day, and so long! True, he had shattered many purposes to reform, but he was sincerely trying again, and he wished his employers to know that he had signed the pledge, and he told one of the gentlemen in the shop what step he had taken. Yes, John B. Gough, slave to rum, could say that he had signed that pledge which might mean emancipation.

"I know you have," was the reply.

"And I mean to keep it," said Gough.

"So they all say, and I hope you will."

Gough re-assured him of his purpose, and said:

"You have no confidence in me, sir."

What an encouraging answer the employer now made!

"None whatever, but I hope you will keep your pledge."

It was not like Joel Stratton's confidence in Gough. He went back to his work. He was discouraged. He saw how he was regarded by others. The sky, that had begun to brighten with a star of hope, was clouding again. While somberly meditating, Gough heard a voice near him. Somebody was speaking to him.

"Good-morning, Mr. Gough," said a gentleman whose approach Gough had not noticed. "I was very glad to see you take the position you did last night, and so were many of our temperance friends. It is just such men as you that we want, and I have no doubt but you will be the means of doing the cause a great deal of good."

The clouds were off the sky and the star of hope was back in its place.

The speaker was a Worcester lawyer, Jesse W. Goodrich. He added, "My office is at the Exchange, Mr. Gough, and I shall be very happy to see you whenever you like to call in—very happy."

Gough had a sensitive nature, and there was a peculiar susceptibility to a kind or an unkind

word at this time. Somebody did care for him,
two, indeed, Mr. Stratton and Mr. Goodrich.
The thought of such kindly interest was as refresh-
ing and reviving as a summer shower to a droop-
ing plant. The book-binder must have held up
his head after that. However, Gough was not
past his troubles yet. Alcohol will not relax its
hold upon its victims easily. There was a fight
before the reformed book-binder. To go without alcohol was a rare thing for him, and the
body burned for the poison that was killing it.
It was death to drink; it must have seemed like
death to stop drinking. Gough went home at
night burdened with a consciousness of some
threatened horror. There was his terrible thirst
which water did not seem to lessen but aggravate.
What he anticipated was another attack of the
horrors. There was a frightful suggestion of it
at the book-bindery. It was the evening suc-
ceeding that of the pledge-signing, and Gough
wished to screw up the press for binding. He
had grasped a bar of iron. Was Gough a magi-
cian? Could he convert iron into flesh and blood,
even slimy flesh and cold blood, a thing that
could twist and try to wriggle away from him,
a snake? He let it go quickly, this repulsive,

8

wriggling snake! Then it changed to iron. There was the bar for screwing up the binding-press. That was all. Gough felt that he was on the edge of a frightful battle, and his fears were realized. When in his chamber he had an awful wrestle with the grim forces of the *delirium tremens*. There were ugly faces, loathsome reptiles, lurid light, blackness, pitiful screams for life. However, he held to his purpose. He fought victoriously the battle. He left the field feeble in body but a conqueror. His health was strengthened, little by little, and the stars of hope in his sky multiplied and brightened.

He spoke again at a temperance meeting, and the impression made was so good that a Mr. Fowler, of Upton, engaged him to give an address. It was about this time that a very important step was taken.

CHAPTER XIII.

A KNIGHT CREATED.

DO we remember what was said about Sand-gate Castle, that old haunt of chivalry by the frothing sea? As our thoughts drift back to the far-away days we recall in imagination the princely displays of gay knight and stately cavalier that old Sandgate must have witnessed. What ceremonies attended the making of those knights I know not, but in the eleventh century a very imposing ceremonial accompanied such an act. In that century, when a person was to be made knight, very serious confession preceded it, and if every candidate frankly and fully told the story of his life the confessional must have echoed to very strange revelations. There was a midnight vigil in church, and we can see the dim, shadowy interior, the tapers faintly burning, and the bowed form of the suppliant candidate. The communion was afterward administered. The warrior presented his sword, which was laid upon the altar. This meant its consecration and

his also to the cause of the Church, and with
this was joined necessarily a resolution to de-
vote himself to a godly life.   A sum of money
must be paid that the sword could be taken from
the altar.   Then a blessing was said over it, and
the highest in the ministry that might be present
girded it about the would-be knight.   His spurs
were also fastened to him.   A blow was now
given him on the shoulder or cheek.   It signi-
fied the last affront he would suffer without any
return for it.   The latter purpose has a strange
sound to ears that have heard the gospel of the
Sermon on the Mount.   Doubtless it is explained
by the after vow which bound him to right
all wrong.   He was pledged to stand up for the
down-trodden against any oppressor, to stand
up for the right, no matter what odds might
be against him, and never, by any act or utter-
ance even, to blot his fair name as a knight or
servant of Christ.   Now let him rise and leave
priest and altar and shadowy church behind him
and go out to put down wrong, and put up the
right, to stand by the side of every weak, assailed,
injured creature.   If he only keep his vow, the
world in such rough, dark days will be rich in
the possession of a pure, strong character.

There is a knight to be created over here in America. It is not the eleventh but the nineteenth century. It is not England, but Massachusetts. We will start in the twilight to find the man. He is in that building ahead. A church? No, only a school-house on so-called Burncoat Plain. We enter, and we confront a crowd packed among the benches, squeezed into corners, sitting anywhere. It is a chilly night, and in the wood stove of a school-house we all know what a fire can be made and is made on raw, bleak days. The big pile of wood furnished by "the deestrick" is close at hand, and carriers of wood abound. The school-house stove is on duty and rapidly warms up to its tropical work. There is the candidate not near any altar, but near that fiery stove. He wears not any gay trappings. He has not been able to buy a decent suit of clothes, and his aged overcoat must do service as a concealer of his shabbiness. This coat-screen comes high up, buttoned to the very chin. He has not brought any sword or any spurs. His is to be a warfare of entreaty and prayer. Like all the knights in such a service, he must go afoot, or in very simple fashion if riding. And the ceremony of knighthood is just—

a talk.   There is no slap on the cheek or shoulder,
though he may expect to get the like sometime,
and all he can do, probably, will be to quietly
stand and submissively take **it.**   There is no
priest to bind sword and spur, and only these
people are here who live in the vicinity of the
school-house on Burncoat Plain.   Plain folks are
here ; not because of their residence in this level
neighborhood, do I mean, but simple, unpretend-
ing, every-day people.   These are anxious to
hear the speech of the new knight, and though
he would like to get away from that fiery stove
the crowd prevent him.   He must stand there,
fire up with his subject, stand also the fire without, and—roast.   It would never do to unbutton
the old overcoat and reveal the sorry condition
of his clothes.   So he speaks on.   He talks
about temperance.   He consecrates himself to
it.   He pledges to do his best for total abstinence.   He urges his hearers also to espouse it.

I do not imagine that John B. Gough had
any idea that in the school-house a knight was
receiving his consecration to temperance.   I do
not think that his spectators, auditors who with
staring eyes and gaping mouths followed him
in the course of his thought down into the shud-

dering depths of drunkenness, then up to the
heights of abstinence, had any idea that these
first efforts of Gough were a divine setting-apart
to a wonderful crusade against rum, that great
despot enslaving so many bondmen. We start
many movements little knowing their significance. When a late Vice-President of the
United States, Henry Wilson, as a young man
came tramping down in his poverty from New
Hampshire to Massachusetts, he did not know it
was the beginning of a march whose last stages
would take him to the chair of the vice-presi-
dency at Washington. He went to work shoe-
making, stuck to it, rose from a shoe-maker's
bench to a legislator's, kept rising, till he occupied
a very lofty chair in the nation's gift.

So we follow our hero in the instance of this
story, from the school-house to another unpreten-
tious place of gathering, where he repeats his
knightly vow of abstinence, where he pledges
himself to the championship of this cause. In
all these places it is a true knighthood that is
espoused ; but who appreciates its significance ?
Our hero himself, John Bartholomew Gough,
knows not what future is before him as he speaks
there by the hot fire in the school-house stove at

Burncoat Plain. He has a story to tell, and he must tell it, not daring in his poverty to lessen his hot discomfort by loosening his overcoat. When he speaks again and again, and makes vows truly knightly, he has no idea that he is consecrating himself to a great world-effort, that the platform will become his triumphant and final field. He wishes to do good, and hopes that his voice may reach some who may need his help.

Let us keep clearly in mind the date of these first efforts, the latter part of the year 1842. Gough was only twenty-five years old. Requests for his services were so numerous that to answer them he asked his employers to allow him to be away a week or two. They consented, and he left on his bench a lot of Bibles. They were not finished, and he never came back to conclude his task. He was now giving almost all his time to his appeals for temperance. His voice was heard ringing out its warnings in many towns in Worcester County. He was soon, though, to run into a very mortifying experience. He was hard at work making temperance addresses. It must not be forgotten that his appetite for liquor, though smothered, was not dead. No one of us can fairly judge the intensity of the rum-thirst unless we have acquired it. It is not a natural appetite. The craving is unnatural and a symptom of disease. That is the work of the poison, alcohol, on the human system. Temperance was up in Gough's brain, but *disease* was still down in his body.

One to whom the care of a widow's son had been committed said that the young man had heard during his educational course that the use of wine was not only proper, but it actually aided the temperance cause. This nonsense the young man accepted as good counsel and acted in accordance with it. A few years went by.

One night, without ceremony, he rushed into the room of the friend in whose care he was once placed and made a sad confession. He said he had been told during his senior year (in college) that it was safe to drink wine. That idea had ruined him. His friend asked if his mother were aware of this. No, she was ignorant of a sin he had solicitously covered up. He was asked if he were such a slave that he could not give up the habit.

"Talk not to me of slavery!" said he. "I am ruined, and before I go to bed I shall quarrel with the barkeeper of the ———— for brandy or gin to sate my burning thirst." In a month this young devotee of alcohol was dead. That is the kind of appetite Gough was fighting with. When he quit drink, whose excitement for years he was familiar with, he missed it. That was not strange when we remember the nature of alcohol.

A writer in the *Union Signal* thus testifies to the strength of Gough's appetite, declaring that "his was a life of fierce conflict," that to "souls it is sometimes given to have the appetite for strong drink taken away, but not so was it with Gough. God saw fit to make him 'perfect through suffering,' and, through unceasing conflict with the old appetite, kept him from forgetting how fierce is the conflict and how alone victory can be won. This is one secret of his power to save men.

*   *   *   *   *   *   *

"About ten years ago an intimate friend of Mr. Gough related to me an incident illustrating this point. They were neighbors, accustomed to go back and forth between each other's houses with very little ceremony. One warm day in summer when the doors stood open, Mr. A. went to Mr. Gough's. His tap on the door not being answered, he walked through the hall into the sit-

ting-room. There lay Mr. Gough stretched out
on the sofa, his face covered with his hands. His
wife sat at the window, apparently reading, but
a glance showed that her paper was upside down,
and there was such a look of agony on her face
Mr. A. exclaimed, 'What is the matter, Mary?'
She made no answer, but Mr. Gough, uncover-
ing his face, stretched out his hand to his friend,
and when Mr. A.'s hand was placed in it, grasped
it like a vise. 'You think I care for you, Edward?' he said. 'You have given me too many
proofs of your affection for me to doubt it,'
replied his friend. 'And you think I love that
little woman sitting over there?' said Mr. Gough,
pointing to his wife. 'I am sure you do, John,
better than your life.' 'Yet,' said Mr. Gough,
and the beaded drops on his forehead told how
great was his agony, 'I would see you both dead
at my feet for the sake of a glass of whisky.'
For hours that awful conflict went on and that
heroic soul battled alone. Friend nor even wife
could enter the conflict with him. Yet not alone
was he. One like unto the Son of God was with
him in the flames and brought him out with not
even the smell of fire upon his garments." *

* *Union Signal*, Gough Memorial, April 8, 1886.

No one believes that Gough would have sacrificed any body that he might gratify his appetite, but this ebullition of desire was a proof of fierce temptation. Let us not then forget how sharp was the craving of Gough for alcohol as we return to watch his early experience. He had a very nervous temperament, and he was working hard in the cause that had saved him and which he knew could save others. He had a list, thirty towns long, recording his future engagements, and he came to Worcester. His head was troubling him. When a boy he met with an accident to his head, and this now gave him trouble. He appeared strangely. His landlady urged quiet upon him and a rest in his bed. Gough's nerves were in such a state that he could not follow the advice comfortably. An unrest drove him from spot to spot. It sent him out of the house, and while a wanderer in the street he heard the station-bell whose ringing warned travelers of the leaving of the train for Boston. Gough had no reason for taking this train. He only had the strange impulse of unrest, and in his uneasiness he took that train. It rumbled off toward Boston and took Gough with it. Alas! it was a ride in the wrong direction.

CHAPTER XIV.

A FALLEN KNIGHT.

WHEN Gough reached Boston he knew not what to do, but purposelessly sauntered through the streets. He thought finally of the theater and went to it. There he met some old associates. Ah, one's old associates—how much good or harm they may do if turning up some unexpected day! Gough's friends observed that he did not act naturally. He could only say that he had a strange restlessness, that he was very sick. They took him to a strange doctor, the keeper of an oyster-room, where Gough's companions not only offered him oysters as medicines, but somebody tendered liquor. Heedlessly Gough took it. When he had drunk it, the ugly conviction visited him that he had broken his pledge. If a pit ever opened before a poor fellow, it yawned then before Gough. Here he had been fighting liquor for five months, gloriously conquering his old enemy, and in an unguarded moment he had soiled the cross upon his breast.

Did the person who pressed Gough to take that glass of liquor know what he was doing? If he did, heavy was his burden of responsibility. He had the spirit of the fiend who tried in the wilderness to overthrow our Saviour's hopes.

Gough had thus met with temptation, and amid circumstances of peculiar peril. The body was weak, he was away from home, he was in an oyster-room and a rum-hole, he was with old companions. Down before this temptation he had gone. One glass opened the gate for the entrance of another. He passed the night in Boston. He awoke in the morning to a painful consciousness of his error in drinking, the night before. What could he do? He left Boston and went to his old place of residence in Newburyport. There the unexpected turns up, as it does sometimes very uncomfortably, just when we are not looking for it. He was asked to speak at a temperance meeting. He was in the depths of remorse now. He did speak, however, and went to Boston again. There he drank once more. He then determined he would go back to Worcester. It was such a sorry traveler who returned in the rumbling cars! But go he must. His friends were wondering what detained him, but he came at last and frankly told the story of his fall. He signed again the pledge, but made up his mind to leave Massachusetts, packing his effects for such a journey. The friend that *sticks* is the friend for a hard place. Gough's supporters proved their sincerity, for they gathered about him and urged him to stay that he might be present at the temperance meeting occurring the night of the day appointed, in his own mind, for his departure. He attended the meeting, spoke, fully acknowledged his fault in his fall, and was moved to tears by the kind reception given him. Gough showed no concealment of his mistakes, but frankly avowed them in a spirit of true penitence, going to the different towns where he had made engagements and acknowledging every thing. A man goes down every time he sins, but he takes one grand step up when he is ready to confess his fault and ask the forgiveness of others. There is nothing unmanly in confession; the lack of manhood is in the sin that makes confession necessary.

With regard to Gough's fall is there any thing about it so very strange? Look back over his struggles to reform, and tell me if one very important source of success in all moral improvement had not been overlooked. Gough had left out God. Where is the story of his surrender to God? Where is it said that through that opened door of submission God had come into his soul to clean out the old evil, to fill that soul with himself, strong, never faltering in effort, victorious? The only wonder is that Gough held out against the enemy as long as he did. In the new reformation that followed, Gough sought help from God.

I have already referred to Gough's kind reception by temperance friends after his fall. It is a divine quality to forgive and forgive readily. If we keep our friends shivering a long time at the door after they have knocked for admission, the chill may provoke them to sinning again. We must trust people. They may do better and they may do worse. We cannot anticipate. They will do their best, though, when they feel that they have our confidence, and they will go into the fight knowing that, though a warm foe may be ahead, there are no lukewarm supporters in the rear.

CHAPTER XV.

LANCE IN REST AGAIN.

OUR knight of temperance went out to do grand service, lecturing in the smaller places, but eventually directing his sharp, brave weapons against the enemy in the great cities. He had a helpmeet to encourage him, and her name must not be omitted here. Rev. Dr. Cuyler says:

"Miss Mary Whitcome, the sweet, fair daughter of a Boylston farmer, consented to marry him during the first year after he signed the temperance pledge in Worcester. In the summer of 1856 I visited Brother Gough at his Boylston home to aid him in revival services which he was conducting in his own church, then without a pastor. He was supply committee, Sunday-school superintendent, pastor, and leader of inquiry meetings, all in himself. One evening he took me to the house of his neighbor, Captain Flagg, and said to me: 'Here in this house Mary and I did our brief two or three

9

weeks of courting. We did not talk love, but
only religion and the welfare of my soul. We
prayed together every time we met, and it was
such serious business that I did not even kiss her
until we were married. She took me *on trust*,
with three dollars in my pocket, and has been to
me the best wife God ever made.'"

Like Mary of old she proved by her life-work
that deep in her heart was planted the element
of consecration.

It is a matter of interest to know just how
Gough appeared in those early days of his career
as a great temperance orator. He is of slight
build, has flashing eyes set in a sad, thin face,
and he has a nervous, intense manner. His voice
has great range of expression. It can flame
out in a righteous indignation or soften to those
inimitable tones of pathos, subduing and melting
the hearts of his hearers. Does he need the
help of satire? His tongue can hiss out a sharp
invective. Would he make his hearers see any
of life's humorous sides? He can imitate the
fuss and fret of the fat old farmer geeing to his
oxen that lazily pull on the old wood-sled, act the
marvel-loving sailor spinning a yarn in the fore-
castle when winds are fair, or the Yankee trader

driving in a rural district a prudent bargain. You can see how the life at Sandgate must have reached forward and influenced him. He is the soldier in a grander army than his veteran father ever saw, and going out to meet the grim forces of King Alcohol. He is the knight riding out of Sandgate Castle with keen lance and sharp sword to strike the enemy wherever he may be found. It is the chivalrous element revived in him, the rising up of a noble, heroic purpose to stand as the stronger on the side of the weaker. His young life among the poor enables him to reach down with tender, sympathizing hands where the lowly are, and then with his inspiriting, noble, hopeful eloquence he can exalt them among the rich of the land. And only the drunkard knows how Gough, through a later experience than boyhood, can come into his dreary soul, sit down there in all the emptiness, gloom, despair, and say, " Brother, I have been in this very place. Let me help you up."

In the humble volume telling of Gough's early years,* I find an account of his appearance in Philadelphia as an orator. It is a sketch by an English traveler and added to the volume as

* *Autobiography*, Boston, 1845, p. 146.

an appendix.   It is January, and the writer,
learning that a young man by the name of Gough,
who has made "quite a sensation," is to speak on
temperance, resolves to hear him.   He finds the
church in which Gough will speak, and it over-
flows with an eager audience.   He goes on to
say : "As seven o'clock drew near every eye was
strained in order to catch the first glimpse of
him.   There was a perfect furor."   It is now
after seven, and the people are uneasy.   "Presently there is a stir near the door, and a grave-
looking, spectacled personage, with hair

> " ' half-way
> On the road from grizzle to gray,'

is seen pushing, with monstrous difficulty,
through the crowd. . . . 'There he goes ! That's
Gough, him with the spectacles on !' whispers
one to another as the grave-looking personage
ascends the steps " of the pulpit. No, that can
not be the orator, they conclude, for he is much
younger.   Then "the sexton, stepping forward to
manage the light, is at first supposed to be Gough.
Finally the orator himself comes.   Every
body whispers to every body else, 'That's him ;'
and this time they are right, for Mr. J. B.
Gough it is.   What, that pale, thin young man

with a brown overcoat buttoned closely up to
his chin, and looking so attenuated that a toler-
ably persevering gust of wind would have had
no difficulty in puffing him to any required
point of the compass—that he who has swayed
multitudes by his oratory, made strong men
weep like little children, and women to sob as
if their hearts would burst? Yes, look at his
large, expressive eyes, mark every feature, and
you see the stamp of no common man there.
The young apostle of temperance is before us."
The lecture is described "as the most awfully
interesting autobiography I ever listened to.
During that week and the week following Mr.
Gough lectured to congregated thousands in
Philadelphia. . . . The excitement was tremendous. . . . Gallery and pulpit-stairs and aisles
were thronged with people of every class."

When Dr. Cuyler made Gough's acquaintance,
the good minister was a student in the seminary
at Princeton, and he speaks of Gough as " in the
early dawn of his splendid fame. His voice had
a sweetness, a tenderness of pathos, a rich compass which hard usage well-nigh destroyed long
ago, and he had already prepared some of his
most powerful scenic descriptions. Gough was

a great dramatic performer, with much of Garrick's talent for impersonating every variety of character. He composed his own dramas, painted his own scenery with the tongue, conducted his own dialogues, and was a whole 'stock-company' in himself. When he came to Princeton and began to mumble over his first apologetic sentences before his cultured auditors they all pitied him; but when he told the pathetic story of 'Luke' and his poor bruised wife, and gave his thrilling description of the *delirium tremens* all the college professors wept like children. The brilliant Professor Dod said to me, 'That man equals De Quincey, the opium-eater, in pictorial power.' Within five years from that time Gough reached the zenith of his fame as an orator. In Cincinnati he had to climb by a ladder into the window of the packed church (following old Dr. Lyman Beecher up the ladder) in order to reach the pulpit. In every city his name was enough to attract thousands who had never heard a syllable in favor of teetotalism before."

Gough did not make the mistake that has trapped some men, cherishing the fancy that he could safely hold on to Christ and yet live outside the fellowship of Christ's Church. He became a member of the Congregational Church on Ashburton Place, Boston, of which the Rev. Dr. E. N. Kirk was pastor. This minister of God was one of great warmth of heart, of ready, outreaching sympathy, and his ministrations were a strong buttress to Gough's principles. While these friends of Gough are mentioned, and he was one to make quickly and long hold his friends, it must not be supposed that he was without his enemies. He fell into one trap, and I will let Dr. Cuyler in his brief but vivid life-sketch of Gough tell the story:

"It was during the summer of 1845 that Mr. Gough's name suffered its only cloud; but that was speedily dispelled. While in a drug-store in New York he carelessly swallowed a glass of soda-water which an enemy had drugged, and under the poisonous influence of which he lay in a stupid debauch for several days. I never shall forget my first interview with him—at the house of Mr. George Hurlburt, on Brooklyn Heights—after he was discovered in a low haunt and rescued. He lifted his head from the pillow and gave me the whole pitiable story of his unintentional fall; and his statement was entirely

corroborated by the examining committee from
Dr. E. N. Kirk's Boston church, to which Mr.
Gough belonged.   That unhappy episode taught
him a salutary lesson of caution, and he was
never 'caught napping' again.   But the old
terrible habit, which was in his system like a
chained tiger, was only kept in subjection by
the omnipotent grace of God.   He confessed to
me again and again that the smell of a teaspoon-
ful of brandy was dangerous to him, and that,
unless the unseen hand of his Saviour held him
fast, he would have been in the gutter forty
years ago."

The unseen hand!   It is our only hope.
Scarred with the red Calvary-sign of God's great
love, let us steadfastly cling to it.

CHAPTER XVI.

GOING TO HEAR GOUGH.

WE are going to hear Gough to-night. Whether he speak in church or hall there will be a crowd. Notice which way the throng in the streets may drift, and follow the drift, and you will reach Gough. When he started out as a lecturer his receipts were scanty, often miserably small, but as he went on, his pockets grew heavier. He could command large audiences, and people would readily pay an admission-fee to hear him. While Gough received large sums for lecturing his expenses were heavy, and he was also a generous giver. Let us go to hear him. Having reached the place where Gough speaks, you must hurry to the seat you would like to occupy or you will find somebody in it unless you have that mortgage-claim upon it, "Reserved seat." Look around and see the kinds of people in the audience. Just before you is a boy, all eyes, save what may be ears and mouth, and on the alert to see

Gough soon as possible, hear all he can, and also gape at him in wonder. The boy is an errand-boy, and before Gough gets through he may have a word to say about "chaps" that run errands, and it will surely interest this auditor.

The man in front of the boy, with a bright, sharp look, as if he were a saw and could cut through any subject set before him, is a scholar of some kind, professor, or college president. He likes to hear Gough because somehow Gough in his wide experience will take this student of books out into the bustling, rushing world. May be he has students under him who may have tripped over the wine-bottle, and he wants to know what Gough may have to say about such unfortunate stumblers. That man at your right is a teamster. He likes to hear Gough because Gough acts out his speeches. "I wouldn't wonder," he says to himself, "if Gough drove a coach-and-four right across the stage, and I want to see him handle the ribbins." That man at your left is a clergyman. He wants to know how to "handle," how to "drive" the temperance work. He says to himself, "May be I shall get, too, from Gough some hint about preaching. They say he is very, even wonderfully natural."

And are not those men up in that corner of the gallery or balcony, just as it may be church or hall, a group of sailors? Yes, the *Sally Ann* arrived in port this morning, and the seamen aboard, finding out that John B. Gough is going to lecture, have come rolling up from the wharf. "They say he knows how to tell about a storm at sea," is their thought, "and we want him to spin just one yarn for us." Ah, Jack, you will have some plain words said to you about grog-drinking, and the storms it can raise, if you stay. You will stay, though, and go away feeling that you have a baby-heart and woman-eyes.

And look down toward the door of the room. You will see, I dare say, men with shadowed faces, men who know about the power of the rum-habit. And all over the audience-room you will find people who for one reason or another have deepest interest of a very practical nature in this subject of temperance. There are wives and mothers whose souls are tormented with fear lest those dear to them may have gone too deep into that Valley of Shadows which might fittingly be termed Death, and yet where those who enter are miserably living on.

But there is Gough, that slender, wiry man,

all nerve, all intense feeling, who has suddenly come from some place in the rear and now confronts his audience. He goes to work at once. It is very direct work in the case of Gough. He gives himself entirely to *you*. He makes you feel that he is personally interested in *you*, not the man away up in Greenland or down in Hottentot-land, but *you*, *you* before him. Gough has a fellow-feeling for every body, loves his kind and likes to be with them. Have you forgotten when he was a drunkard how his social nature took him where people were, out among companions that did him no good? Gough has an interest in every body, in any of the highest as well as the lowest, in Queen Victoria and the boy that blacks boots for Queen Victoria's children.

Gough will make you feel that you are one in a big family gathered all around him, and that he means you as well as your neighbor. He will seem to come down from the platform and get into the seat before you and there talk *to you*. All this you will appreciate. You will also feel that he is thorough, radical, on the temperance question. Moderate drinking will not answer for Gough, you say. Fittingly may be noticed here the experience of the Congressional Temperance Society. It was organized not to stop drinking, but to limit it. It was found, though, that its members when it came to practice did not all believe in fences. The ninth year of its existence it was planted on that safe basis, total abstinence. At a meeting held not long after this change, a speaker, addressing the chair, declared, " Mr. President, the old Congressional Temperance Society has died of intemperance, holding the pledge in one hand and the champagne-bottle in the other." Our present temperance knight could never fight his battles that way. He would never try to fight a champagne-bottle with a champagne-bottle unless he smashed one against the other. People who talk temperance and yet hug the bottle will never rid the land of the curse under which it groans. Gough, to-night, will not permit his hearers to believe they can safely tamper at all with the evil of drink. Can they have one glass? The man before us on the platform knows all about its power. In an address given in 1877 at the twelfth anniversary of the National Temperance Society, New York, Mr. Gough said :

"There are many persons who talk about us as being fanatics. They tell us we are rabid on this subject of temperance. I ask any reformed drunkard in this audience to-night if it is not right to be rabid against an evil that has scorched and blasted and scathed and scarred us, and we shall carry the marks of it to the grave with us. Young men sometimes have an idea that a man can sow his wild oats and get over it. You put your hand in the hand of a giant, and he crushes it. He may tear at your hand, and it may be healed, and by and by in some sort it may be a useful one, but it is a mutilated hand ; its beauty and symmetry have gone forever. We who have passed through this fire know something of its awful scourge ; we know something of the terrible struggle to get out of it. I think we ought to be what they call rabid."

It would be very natural if in any temperance lecture by Gough he illustrated the strength of his appetite for alcoholic beverages. His only safety lay in absolute isolation from all that would intoxicate. At an anniversary address given before the National Temperance Society, from which I have already quoted, Gough spoke about attending a church where the clergyman gave a very moving discourse. Afterward came the administration of the sacrament of the Lord's Supper. Gough referred to the wine used at the communion. He declared, "The very smell of that wine reminded me of days of damning degradation, and I would not have touched my lips to that wine to save my hand from being cut off at the wrist. You well say, 'You are a poor, weak man.' There are multitudes like me. I was conversing with a man from New Hampshire who has done an immense work. He has got over thirty thousand men to sign the pledge, and he said to me, 'I would not dare to put my lips to a drop of wine. Mark me, I am not saying that if I took a glass I should go on drinking. I am not saying what is or is not the strength of my appetite. I say that I cannot consistently swallow alcoholic wine, because it contains the agency and instrumentality that ruined so many.' Do you know what I thought when the cup was handed to me? I looked at it and said to myself, 'There is enough there to ruin me for time and eternity,' and I passed it. I cannot help feeling so upon this subject. I know that a great many persons would criticise me and say I was all wrong."

Gough was right. If there are such temptations incidental to its use, why should alcoholic wine be insisted upon, and especially when the non-alcoholic fruit of the vine is every-where accessible?

But let us turn to the lecturer again and inquire what will be his position when he talks about selling liquor. Thorough there, we may be assured. What does Gough think of those who sell liquor? Shall they be permitted to go on peddling death for five or ten cents a glass? This is what he said at the meeting in 1877, whose utterances I have already noticed:

"When I first began, you know, it was in the height of the Washingtonian movement. It was a grand movement, and many were rescued; still, it did not seem to be all that was desired. At any rate, it was as if we were so horrified at the sight of men going over the rapids and down the awful cataract that we were lining the banks with men and building bridges over the rapids, and as they came down we picked them up and passed them over to friends who bound up their wounds. Still the stream of victims came along in multitudes. We would pick up some whom we picked up six months before as bad and even worse than they had been. The work of saving these men went on gloriously. But by and by we began to investigate. We went above the rapids and there found men whose sole business it was to push them in—to entice them to enter upon that smooth, deceitful stream. We came to the conclusion that, while we manned our forces to save men, we must man other forces to stop the murderous business of inducing men to drink."

Yes, "Stop!" That is what Mr. Gough again and again said; selling must be stopped. Joseph Cook has given us John B. Gough's position in a fervid eulogy pronounced in Tremont Temple, Boston, in February, 1886:

"Let us recollect, therefore, that to John Gough the center of the temperance army was the Church, the right wing the law, the left wing moral suasion; or, if you please to say, the left wing the law, and the right wing moral suasion. He was a broad man; he meant that the whole army should act as a unit; and he found it was none too strong when employed as a single weapon against the most terrific political and social danger of our time."

The crowning glory of Gough's merits as a
10

lecturer was that he so exalted the power of God
to lift the fallen and save the lost.   He could
heartily echo the opinion of a degraded drunkard who said, " When I had become almost a
wreck, both physically and mentally, and friends
had pronounced my case hopeless, then it was
that Jesus came to my rescue and I gave him
my heart.   That saved me."   Gough believed
away down to the bottom of his soul that God
could and would do all that, and people must let
God do it.   Perhaps our lecturer will tell a story
illustrating this point.   His auditors always liked
to hear him tell a story.   I have already said
that—it would be acted.   If he were telling
about a boy selling newspapers, an old toper going up to a bar for his drink, a simpering, silly
woman turning up her nose in disgust at the
temperance reformation, then Gough would
mimic all these acts.   While he exalted the
worth of the Bible and the value of its precepts
as a help to right-doing, he hated shams, and he
was the very man to set off in a ridiculous light
any hypocritical handling of the Scriptures.
" Whisky is your greatest enemy," said a minister to one of his deacons.   " But," said the deacon, " don't the Bible say that we are to love

our enemies?" "O, yes, deacon, but it does not say that we are to swallow them." If Gough were telling that story on the platform he would have acted out that quoter of Scripture in such a sarcastic way that it would have been a severe rebuke to any such irreverent, false use of God's precepts. I find in another lecture before the National Temperance Society a story that Gough used to show our need of and dependence upon the grace of God. Here it is:

"God is the motive power, and our work is simply nothing in comparison with him. Then, as we put forth our efforts, let us make our appeal to him.

"I remember (and I do not know whether it was a legend or not) that a missionary party were passing over the prairie when one of them exclaimed, 'See, see that red glare; what is it?' They looked and watched, and one old trapper, shading his eyes with his hand, cried out, 'The prairie is on fire, and it is spreading at the rate of twenty miles an hour. It will destroy us, and nothing will be left but a few charred bones to tell of the party passing over the prairie.' 'What shall be done?' The trapper cried, 'We must fight fire with fire. Work, work! pull up

the grass; make the circle larger, larger, larger!
Quick, quick! I feel the heat upon my brow!
Quick, for your lives! pull up the grass, pull up
the grass! Now for the matches!'

"They searched and found two. Hastily they
struck one and it failed, utterly failed. One
match, and the fire coming in the distance, leap-
ing with its forked tongues through the dry
grass at twenty miles an hour! Only one match!
The missionary, baring his brow, said, ' God help
us; for thy great name's sake help us in our
extremity.' Every heart prompted the word,
and the lips uttered 'Amen.' They struck the
match; it caught fire, and the grass was ignited,
and, as the fire fenced them in a circle, they
marched on triumphant, exultant, victorious.

"Our instrumentalities—national temperance
societies, bands of hope, sons of temperance,
good templars, whatever they may be—are as
feeble as that one match. Before we put forth
our efforts, then, let us reverently ask God to
help us for his great name's sake, and we, with
those we have worked for, shall stand in the
circle unharmed while the flames play away in
the distance and we stand saved, not by our
own efforts alone, but by our own efforts blessed

and acknowledged by Him in whose hand are the destinies of all men."

You would have been intensely interested in the orator's representation of that prairie-fire incident. You would have seen the old trapper shading his eyes and looking off. You would have seen him pulling grass and scratching one of those two precious matches. Then you would have seen the missionary baring his brow and solemnly appealing to God. Again, the scratching of a match—their last visible source of help—and then you would have witnessed the triumphant upspringing of flames, while round the circle marched the rejoicing survivors.

Will Gough use the temperance pledge to-night? He did give it a very important place in his work. In Cincinnati, during a fortnight's crusade, 7,640 names were attached to the temperance pledge. Three hundred of these were the autographs of college students. Dr. Cuyler said that Gough once showed him several volumes that had over 150,000 signatures! A hundred and fifty thousand! So many streams flowing toward fields blossoming with health, purity, happiness! So many stars hopefully shining and lighting up spaces that without temperance were dark indeed! Some of the streams may have ceased to flow and some of the stars may have gone out, but how many of these influences of hope were continued in useful, happy lives. In using the pledge I can readily imagine what arguments Gough might press home upon his auditors. He might ask them to sign for their own sakes, and he might press home the motive he himself forcibly felt in all his relations to the world—action for another's sake. One mounts to the level of noble Christian principle when as the stronger he remembers the weaker and acts so as to advance the interests of the weaker.

Gough worked very hard in his lectures. He gave himself to his subject and his hearers. He was an electrical battery developing an intense interest, his points sparkling and flashing as he went along. Miss Frances E. Willard says of him:

"That lithe form was always in motion up and down the immense platform; that sallow, bearded face framed in a shock of iron-gray hair was of protean aspect, now personating the drunkard, then the hypocrite, anon the saint. Those restless, eager hands, supple as India Rubber, were always busy, flinging the hair forward

in one character, back in another, or standing it
straight up in a third; crushing the drink fiend,
pointing to the angel in human nature or doub-
ling up the long coat-tails in the most grotesque
climaxes of gesticulation, when, with a 'hop,
skip, and jump,' he proceeded to bring down
the house. Dickens says of one of his humorous
characters that 'his very knees winked;' but
there was a variety and astonishment of expression in every movement of Mr. Gough that literally beggars description. . . . The marvel is
that he lived so long, who gave himself so com-
pletely to his work that at the close of every
lecture his clothes were literally wringing wet,
and hours of attention were necessary to soothe
and recuperate him with food and baths, so that,
long after midnight, he could sleep. For this
purpose some friend always went with him, usu-
ally his wife, that strong, brave, faithful 'Mary,'
in whose praise he could never say enough."

Work pays. The lecturer's efforts were sure
to be rewarded with the intense interest of his
auditors. While we are still gathered in his
presence, look about on those who came with us
to hear "John B. Gough." They are wide-
awake, for they have heard something that per-

sonally interests and steadily holds them. In
that nimble man on the platform telling about
some "little chap" on the street, the errand-boy
has seen himself. The professor has a wide grin
on his face, for he has gone out into the world
with the lecturer and has seen many of its follies
and some of their cures. The teamster has in
some incident caught the clatter of the hoofs of
the horses he wanted to see Gough drive, and
he has often been beating his palms together in
hard applause. The minister has learned something about temperance work, but he has been
laughing so intensely at Gough's witty points
that he has forgotten to study the lecturer's way
of holding an audience. And those sailors—see!
They are up in the gallery still. Their eyes are
wet as if a heavy sea had been shipped and the
spray had filled them. The spray came when
Gough told a touching story about a sailor-boy
dying at sea, away from home. When the lecture is over, the applause of the audience is hearty
and prolonged.

Gough did not always lecture upon temperance. He gave some very entertaining addresses
upon other subjects. It would have been very
strange if he had not, though, introduced his

favorite topic, temperance. Major E. T. Scott speaks of a lecture by Gough upon "Curiosity," adding that "he availed himself of the opportunity to 'lug in a bit of temperance,' as he quaintly remarked." It may be a surprise to some that this king among lecturers had the least uneasiness when he faced an audience, and yet he has left on record an account of the nervousness that might afflict him when he had a speech in anticipation. Public speaking, like all other achievements, has its conditions, and one who desires success must make up his mind to meet those conditions. Does any boy or girl read this who "hates" any thing like a declamation? Men who have been a success in their efforts to reach and arouse the public mind have sometimes given a very interesting statement of their struggles in the direction of oratory. One of America's greatest speakers was Daniel Webster, the son of little but honorable New Hampshire. When Webster was fourteen years old he went to Phillips Academy, Exeter. His biographer, Charles Lanman, says: "Here he was first called upon to 'speak in public on the stage,' and the effort was a failure; for the moment he began he became embarrassed, and

burst into tears.   He could repeat psalms to a
few teamsters at the age of seven, but could not
address an assembly when twice that age.   His
antipathy to public declamation was insurmount-
able, and in bearing testimony to this fact he
once uttered the following words: 'I believe I
made tolerable progress in most branches which
I attended to while in this school, but there was
one thing I could not do—I could not make a
declamation.   I could not speak before the
school. . . .   Many a piece did I commit to
memory and recite and rehearse in my own room
over and over again; yet when the day came
when the school collected to hear the declamation, when my name was called, and I saw all
eyes turned to my seat, I could not raise myself
from it!'"   However, when Daniel Webster laid
down his life-work as an orator he did not lay
it down where he took it up, at the ladder's foot,
but on its topmost round.   Between the first
and the last rounds there was a long interval of
climbing, of hard work.   For the sake of the
young let me earnestly say that we must not
close our eyes to the importance of this fact,
work.   A bar of iron that is worth five dollars
can be turned into horseshoes worth $10.50.

Work longer and harder on that iron bar. You can separate it into needles that will bring you $355. Split it up into the blades of penknives, and your labor will bring you $3,295. Make one more trial. Instead of these horseshoes, needles, or penknives, stretch out the iron into the balance-springs of watches. Your five-dollar bar will net you $250,000. So much for work, work, work. Do not undervalue it. Crown it in your regard; it will crown you with honor. Work helped make our temperance knight.

CHAPTER XVII.

ACROSS THE SEAS.

WE are about to transfer our thoughts to the country of which Sandgate by the sea is a part. Let us inquire about the temperance reformation in England. Conscience there was more drowsy than in America. Great Britain's conscience was almost smothered under a great mass of drink. To-day it is more sleepy than that of America. So hard to give a knock at the door loud enough to arouse the heavy British sleeper, and still there have been notable efforts at knocking attended with a measure of success. A noble temperance reformer was Father Mathew, a priest of the Church of Rome. This big-souled man was born in Ireland, October 10, 1790. He was ordained in 1814. In his first sermon he spoke of the Bible assertion that it is more difficult for a rich man to enter the kingdom of heaven than for a camel to pass through the eye of a needle. He said it was the use of riches, not their possession, that might be harmful. A fat old man, rich, too, said to the young preacher afterward, "Father Mathew, I feel very much obliged to you for trying to squeeze me through the eye of a needle." Father Mathew in his ministry was quickly known as a generous, self-sacrificing, loving man. One of his mottoes was, "A pint of oil is better than a hogshead of vinegar." He was full of good works. Incessant in labor, he loved to say, "Take time by the forelock, for he is bald behind." A warm-hearted Quaker, William Martin, was anxious to see the temperance cause pushed, and the thought in his heart was, "Father Mathew is the man to push this work." Martin and Mathew, two good historical names, were associated together in the oversight of the Cork work-house. Martin, witnessing some distressing case, whose occasion was rum, would say to his associate, "O, Theobald Mathew, if thou wouldst only give thy aid, much good could be done in the city."

What the Quaker said stirred the conscience of the Roman Catholic. Seeking God's guidance, Father Mathew resolved to join and press the work of total abstinence. What would he do next? Hark! There is a knock at William

Martin's door, one April morning, in the good year 1838. When the summons was answered who should be wanted but the Quaker himself by this Roman Catholic priest? Sometimes when any thing special is about to happen, our minds are strongly impressed that way, and the Quaker had an idea that Father Mathew might have temperance on his mind. Off the anxious Quaker started. The priest met the Quaker at the door and said cordially, "Welcome, Mr. Martin! Welcome, my dear friend! It is very kind of you to come to me at so short a notice, and so punctually too."

"I was right glad to come to thee, Father Mathew, for I expected that thou hadst good news for me."

"Well, Mr. Martin, I have sent for you to assist me in forming a temperance society in this neighborhood."

"I know it! Something seemed to tell me that thou wouldst do it at last."

The time for the meeting was selected, and William Martin left, saying, "O, Father Mathew! Thou hast made me a happy man this night."

What a good thing just a push may be!

Behind it, though, was a persistent hand, and above the hand were the heart and brain of a big man. People ridiculed the priest, but the meeting was called, and under the pledge was a name at whose signature, its owner said, "Here goes, in the name of God, Theobald Mathew, C. C., Cove Street, No. 1." Sixty additional signatures were given. Some of God's plantings grow very rapidly, and this movement proved to be a quick-growing, overshadowing tree of blessing. How fast it did put forth branches and spread out its leaves! In three months there were twenty-five thousand pledge-signers; in five months, one hundred and thirty-one thousand; in about nine months one hundred and fifty-six thousand.

When the year 1839 opened its doors there were two hundred thousand signatures to the pledge. Observe now its character: "I promise, with the Divine assistance, as long as I shall continue a member of the Teetotal Temperance Society, to abstain from all intoxicating drinks, except for medicine or sacramental purposes, and to prevent as much as possible, by advice and example, drunkenness in others." That clause, " as long as I shall continue a member of the Teetotal Temperance Society," is not as satisfactory as the simple, absolute promise to abstain—always. This second form of promise is a road long enough to reach across life, which is the thing desired. Better journey in Father Mathew's shorter road than not to travel at all. A vast host made this journey. The work spread. The movement was too big to be *corked* up in Father Mathew's city and its neighborhood. The great reformer went to Limerick, and there, in the course of four days, one hundred and fifty thousand signed his pledge. Waterford only needed three days to add eighty thousand to the list. Maynooth made a contribution of thirty-five thousand, varying the usual quality of signatures with those of eight professors and two hundred and fifty students. In two days Galway furnished a hundred thousand names. "The form of the engagement partook of the religious," it is said. A medal was given, and the signer greatly revered the little memorial. In some minds the idea gained ground that this "Apostle of Temperance" enjoyed Heaven's smile, and that he was miraculously aided. Ireland's habits were so much affected that many breweries and distilleries were closed. Spiders

were the busiest creatures in those dingy build-
ings. It was a happy state of things. A wealthy
distiller once asked Father Mathew how he
could ruin the business of so many people. So
Father Mathew told him this story: "A fat
duck who had filled her crop with worms was
met by a fox. Sir Reynard was going to make
a meal of the duck, when she asked him how he
could take the life of a harmless duck just to
satisfy hunger. 'Out upon you, madam!' said
the fox. 'With all your fine feathers you are a
pretty thing to lecture me about taking life to
satisfy hunger. Is not your crop now full of
worms? You destroy more lives in one day to
satisfy your hunger than I do in a whole month.'"
Was not that a good answer to a distiller with
his stuffed crop, stuffed with the money of poor
people? With this decrease in liquor-drinking
went a decrease of crime.

Father Mathew's work could not be confined
to Ireland. He went to England in 1843. Here
six hundred thousand entered into covenant with
him to let rum alone. In 1849 he came to the
United States. Remaining two years in this
glorious work, though death was trying to stop
him with its attacks of paralysis, he visited

11

twenty-five States, and in three hundred cities administered the pledge. One day this work apparently was all over. He who had been able to say, " I am the strongest man in Ireland," lay in the silence and stillness and helplessness of death ; but what a work he had wrought ! What an influence he left behind to work on for him ! No, death could not stop his influence. In the next life his glorious energy was continued in other forms of blessed activity.

Crossing the Atlantic, we visited Ireland first. Now let us go farther and notice England, and then we will look over the border into Scotland. I give only one name now, the most prominent in England's pioneer temperance movement, Joseph Livesey, born March 5, 1794, in the neighborhood of Preston. He was a poor boy, a weaver, ambitious to know something. He would read and weave at the same time. " For hours I have done this," he says, " and without making bad work. The book was laid on the breast-beam, with a cord slipped on to keep the leaves from rising, head, hands, and feet all busy at the same time. I had a restless mind, panting for knowledge and incapable of inaction. That part of the loom and the wall nearest my seat was covered with marks which I had made to assist me to remember certain facts, and these hieroglyphics were there when I left." It was a cellar whose humble wall witnessed such pathetic efforts to obtain knowledge. "At night," he says, "I was allowed no candle, and for hours I have read by the glare of the few embers left in the fire-grate, with my head close to the bars." One sad feature of his surroundings was that of drunkenness. This is what he said of the church: "We had a sad lot connected with the church. The grave-digger and his father were both drunkards. The ringers and singers were all hard drinkers, and I remember the singers singing in my father's kitchen on a Christmas morning in a most disgraceful condition. The parish clerk was no exception. When the clock-hands were motionless in the morning for want of winding, as was often the case, the remark was, 'The clerk was drunk again last night.'"

Those distant days were dark indeed. Joseph, fortunately, rose above his surroundings. Aptness and study will carry one ahead. In 1831 he took his last glass. He says: "It was only one glass of whisky and water. I often

say it was the best I ever drank—the best because it was the last—and if I remain in my
senses I shall never take another. I did not
then understand the properties of alcoholic liquors, though I ought to have done, being thirty-
seven years of age." That one glass, to use his
own words, "took hold of me. I felt very
queer as I went home, and retired to bed unwell.
Next morning my mind was made up, and I
solemnly vowed that I would never take any intoxicating liquors again—a vow which I have re-
ligiously kept to the present time. I had a large
family of boys, and this resolution was come to,
I believe, more on their account than from any
knowledge I had of the injurious properties of
the liquors." One good step leads to another.
Get the muscles into position for climbing up
one step and they will be very likely to climb
another.   As adults had no opportunity for Sunday-school instruction, Livesey's benevolent, energetic nature made room for that opportunity,
and, New Year's day, 1832, in his adult school
he advised the young men to start a temperance
organization. This was a one-legged affair, as it
permitted the moderate use of malt liquors;
spirits must be abstained from. In other words,

I should say it allowed a man to play with a little powder but not with dynamite. This little-powder business did not work. One day Livesey saw one "John King," of whom he said, "I asked him if he would sign a pledge of *total* abstinence; to which he consented. I then went to the desk and wrote one out. He came up to the desk and I said, 'Thee sign first.' He did so, and I signed it after him." It is claimed that from this fountain-head ran the good, clean, healthy current of the total abstinence movement in England.

There was an old cock-pit in the neighborhood. Its name tells its character. There was room in this chivalrous institution for the brutalizing of seven hundred people, but one September day the cock-pit was used for a refining purpose. There was no cock-fighting at this meeting, but, after a healthy strife over the question of moderation or total abstinence, seven men signed this pledge: "We agree to abstain from all liquors of an intoxicating quality, whether ale, porter, wine, or ardent spirits, except as medicines." This bridge went away over the waters of difficulty, and did not leave any body floundering in temptation when half across. We may have

wondered where the word "teetotal" took its
rise.   It was at a meeting held about this time
that the word was originated, its first letter being
repeated in the pronunciation.   A man who
took such a pledge was not only "total" in his
adhesion to the cause, but "t—total."   One
Richard Turner is said to have originated this
popular term.   On his grave-stone you will find
these words: "Beneath this stone are deposited
the remains of Richard Turner, author of the
word 'teetotal' as applied to abstinence from all
intoxicating liquors, who departed this life on
the 27th day of October, 1846, aged fifty-six
years."   Richard Turner's little flag has led
many to victory.   Joseph Livesey believed in the
printing-press, and he used it in various ways,
publishing the *Preston Guardian* and scatter-
ing temperance documents thick as the leaves
that the autumn-winds rattle down from the
trees.   He wrote, he lectured, he—lived.   He
died in 1884, but lives on, his memory a beacon-
light to many imperiled souls on life's sea.

Up in Scotland a good work was wrought for
temperance by Dr. Thomas Guthrie, good
Thomas Guthrie, whose face has such a sharp,
shrewd, human look—a face that dogs would

run toward, recognizing a friend, but a face that
rogues would run from, knowing a quick-witted
enemy was there.   This Presbyterian clergyman was born in 1803.   In 1837 he went to
Edinburgh, there laboring for his Master.   He
saw down into the depths of the poverty that,
shivering in winter and hungry always, is massed
in the great cities.   He was an eloquent pleader
for ragged schools and total abstinence.   Among
other things influencing him to abstain from
liquor was a half-ragged carman's answer when
Dr. Guthrie was traveling in Ireland.   This carman, in wet, chilly, sticky weather, was offered
a glass of toddy.   He refused.   " I am an abstainer and will take no toddy," said the carman.
" Well, that stuck in my throat," said Dr. Guthrie, " and it went to my heart and (though in
another sense than drink) to my head.   That
and other circumstances made me a teetotaler."

What a picture this is which he paints in dark
colors in his book, *The City : its Sins and Sor-
rows*.   Dr. Guthrie says : " Look at the case of
a boy whom I saw lately.   He was but twelve
years of age and had been seven times in jail.
The term of his imprisonment was run out, and
so he had doffed his prison garb and resumed

his own. It was the depth of winter, and, having neither shoes nor stockings, his red, naked feet were upon the frozen ground. Had you seen him shivering in his scanty dress, the misery pictured in an otherwise comely face, the tears that dropped over his cheeks as the child told his pitiful story, you would have forgotten that he was a thief, and only seen before you an unhappy creature more worthy of a kind word, a loving look, a helping hand than the guardianship of a turnkey and the dreary solitude of a jail. His mother was in the grave, his father had married another woman. They both were drunkards. Their den, which is in the High Street—I know the place—contained one bed, reserved for the father, his wife, and one child. No couch was kindly spread for this poor child and his brother—a mother's son then also immured in jail. When they were fortunate enough to be allowed to be at home, their only bed was the hard, bare floor. I say fortunate enough, because on many a winter night their own father hounded them out. Ruffian that he was, he drove his infants weeping from the door to break their young hearts and bewail their cruel lot on the corner of some filthy stair, and sleep away the cold, dark hours as best they could, crouching together for warmth like two houseless dogs."

Is it any wonder that Dr. Guthrie lifted his voice and cried for total abstinence? Thank God, there were echoes to his cry. Other men cried with him, and Scotland heard a chorus in response.

CHAPTER XVIII.

AN ATTACK ON ENGLAND'S DRAGON.

IT is now 1853. Let us imagine ourselves over in England, packed with many, many others into Exeter Hall. It is a big audience. They were so eager to see somebody and hear something that people waited four hours for the opening of the doors. It is an English audience, solid, hearty, made up of people from varied walks in life. By the side of Tom the plowboy, I can see Smith the grocer, and the "squire" has come from his old-time manor to sit by the side of his village parson. It is a big audience gathered under the auspices of the London Temperance League. It is a smiling, eager, expectant crowd. I seem to hear the whispered inquiries, "Has he come?" "Is he on the platform?" "Where is he?" Who is this "he?" What does it mean? Why, Britain, awakened on the subject of temperance, enjoying the fruits of the labors of men like Father Mathew, Joseph Livesey, Dr. Guthrie, and others, has sent over to America for help in attacking anew that ugly dragon, Drink, still ravaging among them. An American crusader has been invited and has promised to come. This strong, gallant knight may be expected any moment to step upon the platform, and then what a hospitable, welcoming tumult there will be in Exeter Hall!

But who shall it be? What great, strong, stalwart, giant American shall come? Ah, there is America's knight on the platform! What, that slender man before the great congregation? Who is it? Hold! Do you not recognize him? Do you not recall the little fellow from Sandgate on board the packet, the boy with swollen eyes and thumping heart, crying in his homesickness? Do you not remember the young fellow singing comic songs at the theater, singing in the midst of a drunkard's wretchedness? Can you not see the young book-binder going down into the depths of drunkenness at Newburyport? Can you not call back out of the past the poor inebriate that Joel Stratton tapped on the shoulder, and then that temperance knight set apart to his work in such humble gatherings as that in the little school-house on the plain, soon falling before his old

enemy, yet rising again and going out now in
God's strength to do battle every-where in a
glorious cause? Yes, it is Gough who has come
over the seas, and just as St. George gave the
dragon such a worsting, so our knight in God's
name will ride hard on that old beast, Drink.
There he is on the platform, still young, only
thirty-six, the same wide-awake, magnetic Gough.
Not a very big knight! Will *he* ride down the
dragon? The people are applauding, determined
to cheer their idea, whether their ideal may have
arrived or not. And Gough—he is trying to
face composedly this immense sea of enthusiasm
whose waves are running so high. Will he meet
their expectation?

The same oratory, though, that had faced triumphantly great, critical audiences in America is
successful in England. Now Gough bears his
auditors away in some magnificent apostrophe to
temperance, or he leads them captive and in
tears as he descends into the pitiful depths of
shame and misery opened by intemperance, and
tells all to look about them. This moment they
are laughing at some droll mimicry; the next
they flame with him into a burning indignation
at the cruelty of the dragon, Drink. Ah, it is

the same Gough in Exeter Hall, London, as in Tremont Temple, Boston, with the same rare voice and the same rare powers behind it, leading many aroused souls after him as he rides against the dragon.   For this knight from America, Exeter Hall has only enthusiastic admiration.

Gough's platform career in England was one extended triumph.   He was absent in England two years, pleading continually for his beloved cause.   In 1857 he went again to fight that old enemy, Intemperance, on British shores. In 1878 he once more crossed the waters, and when he disembarked at Liverpool what a very complimentary document was handed him !   It was a roll of teetotalers one hundred thousand strong !   He noticed a decided change of opinion upon the subject of temperance.   At a Gough memorial service in Worcester, in 1886, Judge Aldrich is reported as saying of Gough that "in 1878, when about to go to England for the last time, he was given a Godspeed in Mechanics' Hall, and he then stated that when he went to England twenty-five years before not a clergyman of note could be found to preside at his meetings. When he went in 1878, bishops, clergymen, dignitaries, high officials, and even the prime minister vied with each other to do him honor."

Did the once poor boy from Sandgate forget his old home? He remembered it, and went there, speaking to the villagers on his thirty-seventh birthday, and the old scenes were revived. He searched out the motherly old woman who comforted him with milk and ginger-bread when starting on his journey from home, and he made her a handsome gift, calling it a payment, and afterward at Christmas-time he sent her each year fifty dollars. Gough had a long, grateful memory, and here is the place to say that soon after a return to America his old friend, Joel Stratton, died, and Gough each year gave Mrs. Stratton three hundred dollars.

Knowing Gough's energy, the intense sympathy of his nature with every good cause that he represented, we know that those English trips must have been the occasion of abundant labors. I find in some of Gough's own statements a glass through which we can look afar and see this busy knight riding hard and riding ever. Here is a work on *Drinking Usages of Society.** I open it and I see a lecture pronounced by

* Published by Massachusetts Temperance Society, 1861.

Gough at a reception given him in Tremont Temple, Boston. I am about to give an extract. It is a glass that shows our knight on the Glasgow field where the forces of intemperance are massed in strong, deep lines.

At that reception, September 17, 1860, this was said : "Last November, I had spoken in the City Hall of Glasgow to twenty-five hundred people. I was staying at the house of one of the merchant princes of that city, and when we came down-stairs his carriage was at the door—silver-mounted harness, coachman in livery, footman in plain clothes. You know it is seldom teetotal lecturers ride in such style, and it is proper, therefore, that we should speak of it when it does happen, for the good of the cause. As we came down, the gentleman said to me, 'It is so drizzly and cold you had better get into the carriage and wait until the ladies come down.' I think I never had so many persons to shake hands with me. 'God bless you, Mr. Gough!' said one. 'You saved my father!' 'God bless you!' said another. 'You saved my brother!' Said a third, 'God bless you! I owe every thing I have in the world to you!' My hands absolutely ached as they grasped them one after another. Finally, a poor, wretched creature came to the door of the carriage. I saw his bare shoulder and naked feet; his hair seemed grayer than mine. He came up, and said, ' Will you shake hands with me?' I put my hand into his hot, burning palm, and he said, ' Don't you know me?' ' Why,' said I, ' isn't your name Aiken?' ' Yes.' ' Harry Aiken?' ' Yes.' ' You worked with me in the book-binder's shop of Andrew Hutchinson, in Worcester, Massachusetts, in 1842, didn't you?' ' Yes.' ' What is the matter with you?' ' I am desperately poor.' I said, ' God pity you; you look like it!' I gave him something, and obtained the services of Mr. Marr, the secretary of the Scottish League, to find out about him. He picks up rags and bones in the streets of Glasgow, and resides in a kennel in one of the foulest streets of that city. When the ladies came to the carriage and got in, I said, ' Stop, don't shut that door! Look there at that half-starved, ragged, miserable wretch, shivering in the cold and in the dim gaslight! Look at him!' The ring of that audience was in my ears, my hands aching with the grasp of friendship from scores, my surroundings bright, my prospects pleasant, and I said, ' Ladies, look there! *There am I, but for the temperance movement!* That man worked with me, roomed with me, slept with me, was a better workman than I, his prospects brighter than mine. A kind hand was laid on my shoulder, in Worcester Street, in 1842; it was the turning-point in my history. He went on. Seventeen years have passed, and we meet again, with a gulf as deep as hell between us!' I am a trophy of this movement, and I thank God for it."

Hear Gough again in the same lecture:

"A man came to me at Covent Garden, summer before last, and said, 'Mr. Gough, I want you to come into my place of business.' I replied, 'I am in a little hurry now.' 'You *must* come into my place of business!' So, when he got me there—into a large fruit-stall, where he was doing business to the amount of two hundred and fifty or three hundred pounds (a thousand or twelve hundred and fifty dollars) a week—he caught hold of my hand, and said, 'God bless you, sir!' 'What for? Have I ever seen you before?' 'I heard you, sir,' he said, 'in Exeter Hall, in 1853; I was a brute.' 'No, you were not.' 'Well, I was worse.' 'No, you were not.' 'Well, I was as bad as ever I could be.'

12

Then he told me some sad things, and went on: 'God bless you, sir! See what a business I am doing! Look here! See that woman in the corner; it is my wife. La! how I have knocked her about! Would you go and shake hands with her?'

"'I have no objection.'

"'Do, sir.'

"I went up to her and offered my hand. She held back, and said, 'My fingers are so sticky with the fruit, sir!'

"'La!' said the husband. 'Mr. Gough, you don't mind a little sticky finger?'

"'No, sir;' and I shook hands with her.

"Our fingers stuck together! They were more sticky than I had expected. Again the man said to me, 'God bless you, sir! I wish I could give you something. Do you like oranges?'

"'Sometimes.'

"He went to a shelf that was full of them, and began to fill a great bag with them.

"'That's enough, sir;' but he paid no attention to me, but filled the bag and put it in my arms.

"'Go along with you!' said he. 'Don't say a word; go along with you! God bless you!'

" I had positively to hire a cab to enable me to get home !

" The day before Christmas I took an American lady—who is in this house to-night—to see this man, saying, 'I am going to call on a gentleman whom I want you to see.'

" I had spoken on the preceding Monday evening in Exeter Hall for the eighty-first time, and you know when a man speaks eighty-one times in one place on the same subject he gets pretty well pushed for matter; so I told this story there. The first thing he said, when I entered his place of business, was, ' O, you did give somebody a terrible rub last Monday; didn't you?' 'You didn't mind it?' 'Mind it? No; I *liked* it. The man next to me kept a-nudging me and saying, "That means you." But, Mr. Gough, just look at that cellar!' 'I see the cellar.' 'I want to show you this letter. I have a letter from Manchester ordering me to send them five hundred pounds of fruit. Now, do you suppose any body would have ordered that of such a fellow as I used to be? Look at that cellar! I spent a whole Sunday in that cellar on a heap of rotten vegetables, with a rope to hang myself by!

I heard the bells chime for church and knew
when they were singing and when they were
praying and when they were preaching. They
little thought a poor wretch was down here
fighting, for it was a steady fight all that day
between that rope and me and my conscience.
Now, sir, I lease that cellar and clear a hundred pounds a year. Here come my children,
just from boarding-school—four of 'em. Shake
hands with 'em. O, how I wish you lived
where I do!' "

These incidents give just a hint of Gough's
usefulness in connection with his labors in
Great Britain. Told in his unique way, his
flexible voice adapting itself to every turn of
feeling, his face, his form, the whole Gough
thrown into the expression of every character
introduced, and you can imagine the effect on
any audience. And to show the deep resources
of the man, his great bulk of power in reserve,
think of him speaking in one place for the
eighty-first time! Gough made this statement in 1860. He was in Great Britain after
this, and doubtless spoke again in Exeter Hall.
Mr. Cook says that Gough spoke in that grand,
historic place ninety nights in succession.

I thought I had finished, yet I am tempted to give one more extract from that same lecture. This incident specially shows what a hand-to-hand fight our temperance knight carried on with the dragon, Drink. Says Gough: "I spoke in Dundee to the outcasts of that town. . . . It was a horrid sight to look at—rags, filth, nakedness—a festering, steaming mass of putrefying humanity. A woman sat at my feet, and the place was so crowded that I touched her. Her nickname for years had been 'Hell-fire.' The boys called her 'Fire.' . . . Fifty-three times had she been convicted, and sentenced for from six days to four months' imprisonment."

To shorten the lecturer's account, "Fire" was a dreadful woman, a blasphemer, a fighter, a drunkard. He pictured vividly what drink will do.

Some of his auditors "lifted up their naked arms and said, 'O, that is all true.' By and by the woman at my feet looked up and said, 'Where did you learn all that?' Then she looked as if she had some important communication to make to the people, and she said, 'The man kens all about it. Would you give the likes o' me the pledge?'

"'To be sure I will,' said I.

"'O, no, no!' said some. 'It won't do for her to take the pledge.'

"I said, 'Why not?'

"'She can't keep it.'

"'How do you know?'

"'She will be drunk before she goes to bed to-night.'

"'How do you know? Madam,' I said to her, 'here is a gentleman who says you cannot keep the pledge if you sign it.'

"The woman flew into a rage. Said I, 'Before you fight about it, tell me can you keep it?'

"The reply was, 'If I say I *will*, I can.'

"I said, 'Then you say you will?'

"'I will.'

"'Give me your hand.'

"'I will.'

"'Then,' said I, 'put down your name.'

"After she had done it, I said, 'Give me your hand again.'

"She did so, and said, 'I will keep it.'

"'I know you will,' I said, 'and I shall come back again to see you.'

"'Come back when you will,' said she, 'and you will find I have kept it.'"

Some three years after, Gough went back, and the woman had kept her pledge, no longer "Fire," but "Mrs. Archer, a very respectable Scotchwoman." She said to him, "I am a poor body—I dinna ken much, and what little I did ken has been about knocked out of me by the staves of the policemen. They pounded me over the head, sir—I dinna ken how to pray—I never went to God's house these twenty-eight years. I cannot pray, but sometimes I dream," and then her eyes filled—"I dream I am drunk, and I cannot pray; but I get out of my bed, sir, and I kneel by the side of it, and I never get back to it until day-dawn, and all I can say is, 'God keep me! I canna get drunk any more.'" Gough affirmed, "That woman is now to be seen going every day to hear God's word preached."

That was a beautiful forget-me-not, a fragrant souvenir of Gough's activity. Let me pluck another fair flower of remembrance.

Dr. William M. Taylor was at a temperance meeting in England when Mr. Gough was making his third trip to that country. Dr. Taylor said that after the meeting forty or fifty persons came forward and blessed Gough because twenty years before he had saved them from intemper-

ance.   I can see them eagerly reaching out their
hands.   They were not hands pitifully extended
for help, thrust up out of the depths of shame
and sin and weakness, but hands reached down
from heights of grateful triumph and joy, to
which they had been raised by this rescuer from
the abysm of intemperance.

CHAPTER XIX.

SUNSET-TIME.

THE hours through the day may seem to be long, but the trailing shadows of the sunset will fall at last. After the sowing of the spring, month after month must roll by, but the autumn-time will surely come. The yellow grain will be reaped. The harvester will homeward go. That young Sandgate pilgrim, whom we watched as he crossed the seas and began life here, was an old man at last. The time of the sunset was at hand. The harvest-field of this life must soon be left behind. And yet, though an old man, John B. Gough did not relinquish that sphere of effort in which he had been so successful, the platform. His lectures on various subjects still magnetized the people. When Gough spoke, large audiences gathered. He had a list of lectures on popular subjects. Such themes as " Peculiar People," " Fact and Fiction," " Habit," " Curiosity," " Circumstances," were the garb in which he arrayed some of his thoughts and then marched upon the platform these pilgrims of the hour. When he touched on temperance, his soul kindled like tinder meeting a spark. He had his seasons of rest in his home at Hillside, in Boylston, Massachusetts, six miles from Worcester. Its surroundings were picturesque. Within was a tasteful retreat where were clustered various mementoes of his eventful life. He had an excellent library, and it gave him an opportunity to recall his old craft and clothe anew in finer dress many of his volumes.

There was such a contrast between the want, the struggle, the fight of his early days, and the affluence, ease, and victory of his old age. His lectures were exceedingly remunerative. He was enabled thereby to give generously and live in comfort. His last days still found him at work, a reaper in life's great harvest-field. John B. Gough did not own a rusty sickle.

The end came at Philadelphia, in the sixty-ninth year of his age. He was addressing an audience and had uttered the characteristic words, "Young man, keep your record clean!" It was his final appeal. In the far-away Sandgate days, he received a blow on the head from a spade. The blow seemed to be repeated in the darting pains sometimes afflicting him in after years, and he would raise his hand to his head to soothe it. At Philadelphia the hand was going up to stay the pain, when it helpless-ly fell. He too dropped. It was not, though, the blow from a hostile force. It was only the hand of Providence checking him in his earthly course and turning him aside to one still better. He was stricken Monday, February 15, 1886. He died the following Thursday. To the funeral at Hillside many loving hearts hastened and there gathered in a tearful hush around the hon-ored remains. One very touching memento hung across a chair near the coffin in the Hill-side library. It was a little handkerchief brought to Mrs. Gough by a woman who wished the tem-perance advocate to have some pledge of her gratitude. Said this woman:

"I am very poor; I would give him a thou-sand pounds if I had it, but I brought this. I married with the fairest prospects before me, but my husband took to drinking, and every thing went. Every thing was sold, until, at last, I found myself in a miserable room. My hus-band lay drunk in the corner, and my sick child lay moaning on my knee. I wet this handkerchief through with my tears. My husband met yours. He spoke a few words and gave a grasp of the hand, and now for six years my husband has been all to me that a husband can be to a wife. I have brought your husband the very handkerchief I wet through that night with my tears, and I want him to remember that he has wiped away those tears from me, I trust in God, forever."

Gough had said of this handkerchief, "You do not think it worth three cents, but you have not money enough to buy it from me."

The funeral services were without ostentation, but they were very sincere, and hearts far and near were in sympathy. Winter was still on the land when the body of John B. Gough was laid away to rest. Snow still draped the northern hills, and nature, like the orator, seemed dead. But spring was not far away. The buried forces of nature were sure soon to have their resurrection and come forth amid all the beauty and song of a new world. There is no such catastrophe as death to a soul like that of John B. Gough.

I recall his life of marvelous activity that gathered over eight thousand audiences, met over eight millions of auditors, and to see them face to face he was a pilgrim with a record of half a million of miles of travel. By means of his books, as well as his addresses, he found and captured audiences every-where. It has been claimed that over a million copies of his lectures have been sold, and over a hundred thousand of his autobiography. His last book, *Platform Echoes*, had a very flattering reception. In all these ways the fervid, magnetic orator still speaks. While in his handling of many themes he has flashed sparkles out of them, making his discussions both useful and entertaining, his greatest measure of influence accompanies that noble cause of which he once said, " While I can talk against the drink, I'll talk, and when I can only whisper, I'll do that, and when I can't whisper "—what then would he do ? " I'll make motions. They say I'm good at that ! "

Can such a spirit be written down as dead ?

He is God's true knight of temperance, still living, still riding against the foe, still striking hard and smiting sore that ugly dragon, Drink.

THE END.